ESTORIL
BALLET
1

Ever since she was very small, Drina Adams has wanted to be a ballet dancer. Drina is an orphan, and her grandmother disapproves of her interest, so it's hard to find a way to have the ballet lessons she needs. But Drina was born to dance, and this is the story of how she found out the truth about her background, and how she began her career.

These entirely new editions of the Drina ballet books will be eagerly welcomed by young ballet fans everywhere. Drina – whose real name is Andrina Adamo – is a highly realistic heroine, whose struggles to become a dancer are traced through this series of books.

**The Drina books:**
Ballet for Drina
Drina's Dancing Year
Drina Dances in Exile
Drina Dances in Italy

# To

## Kathryn and Nicola Sak

### in the hope that they will like the Drina Books

# Ballet for Drina

by
**Jean Estoril**

Macdonald

J- 1

Text supplied by arrangement with John Goodchild Publishers.
Design by Ewing Paddock.
Illustrations by Jenny Sanders, who would like to acknowledge the
help of Cathy Marston, the young dancer, and her teacher Maureen
Mitchell, of the Eden Dance Centre in Cambridge.

**A Macdonald Book**

First published in Great Britain by
Hodder & Stoughton Ltd

This edition published in 1987 by
Macdonald & Co (Publishers) Ltd
London & Sydney

Set in 11 point Palatino by
🅰Tek Art Limited, Croydon, Surrey
Printed and bound in Great Britain by
Robert Hartnoll (1985) Ltd, Cornwall

Macdonald & Co (Publishers) Ltd
Greater London House
Hampstead Road
London NW1 7QX

A BPCC plc company

**British Library Cataloguing in Publication Data**

Estoril, Jean
    Ballet for Drina. – Rev. ed. – (Drina
    books)
    Rn: Mabel Esther Allan I. Title
    II. Series
    823'.914[J]    PZ7

    ISBN 0-356-11983-1
    ISBN 0-356 11984 X Pbk

# CONTENTS

BOOK ONE
**"I Want to be a Dancer!"**

Drina's New Friend 9
Jenny Talks of Ballet 19
The Watcher in the Ballet Class 30
At the Grand Theatre 43
Purely for Pleasure 54
Christmas 61
"The Changeling" 71
Drina's Triumph 79
Goodbye to the Selswick School 91

BOOK TWO
**Dance to your Shadow**

Drina in London 101
Ballet Books and a Stranger 110
In the Fog 120
Drina's Double Life 130
The Christmas Play 139
Unexpected Meeting 149
Two Tickets for Covent Garden 159
The Whole Truth 167

# BOOK ONE
## "I Want to be a Dancer!"

# 1
# Drina's New Friend

Drina danced for the first time when she was five
years old. Really danced, that is. Before that she
had been aware of music as something to move to and
had often been found by her grandmother moving her
arms and swaying her thin little body in time to a
compelling rhythm.

Then, on her fifth birthday, she heard the first
movement of Mozart's *Eine Kleine Nacht Musik* on the
radio and her grandmother, Mrs Chester, went into the
sitting-room to find her leaping and twirling on the
smooth block floor, her straight black hair flying out in
a cloud and her pale little face absolutely intent. She
did not even notice her grandmother in the doorway,
for she was entirely given over to the dance that she
was creating.

It was only when Mrs Chester crossed rather
abruptly to the radio and switched it off that Drina
came back to earth.

"Oh, Granny, I was making a dance! Don't turn it
off. See! I was a leaf in a wood, whirling down and
then blown by the wind. It was dark in the wood;
nearly dark, and –"

"I've put the candles on your cake," Mrs Chester
said, very kindly but firmly. "Come and see if you like
it."

Drina was little more than a baby then, but she was quick for her age and she knew very well that she had displeased her grandmother, but it was difficult to know how. It was only very rarely that Mrs Chester was cross with her about anything, for she was inclined to spoil her orphaned granddaugher. Mr Chester was just the same, though Drina did not see nearly so much of him. He was manager of an important firm of manufacturers in the Midland town where they lived, and his work involved much travelling. But when he was home, in the evenings before Drina went to bed, and sometimes at weekends, he gave her his whole attention.

So Drina stood stock still in the middle of the sitting-room, her arms gradually falling to her sides and the dreamy look fading from her face.

"I was only dancing," she said, in a puzzled voice, and Mrs Chester suddenly gathered her in her arms; a most uncharacteristic gesture. She was deeply fond of Drina, but she was not at all demonstrative by nature.

"I know. And dancing very nicely. But there are plenty of other things besides dancing. Birthday cakes, for instance. Come and see!"

So Drina went to see the birthday cake and duly admired the five pink candles, but she was left with a dim impression that her grandmother had not liked to see her being a leaf in a twilit wood.

It was to be an impression that grew as the years passed, though it was no more than a feeling, a faint knowledge, at the back of her mind. At seven, Drina asked if she could go to a dancing class with some of her friends and was refused.

"You've got so many other things to do," Mrs Chester said firmly. "And you're not very strong, you know. I don't want you to worry about it, Drina dear,

but the doctor would like you to be out of doors as much as possible. Perhaps you can have dancing lessons when you're older. We'll have to see. But by then I expect you'll be wanting to learn to skate, or ride a horse, or one of a dozen other things."

Drina was secretly absolutely sure that she would still want to learn to dance, even though it might be fun to learn to skate and ride, but she said no more. When her grandmother's kind, rather worn face looked like that, she knew better than to bother her.

Only a short while later, she was watching the television before going to bed and, just as she was growing sleepy and her attention was beginning to wander, she stiffened into sharp awareness. For the screen graceful, white-clad figures were dancing – dancing, too, as she had never imagined. It was perfect! So perfect that quick tears stung her eyes.

Mrs Chester, who had been sorting some papers at her desk at the other end of the room, came towards her.

"Time you went up, Drina. It's past your bedtime, and it isn't good for you watch television for too long."

"But what is it?" Drina demanded, blinking away the tears in a shamefaced way. "Oh, please let me stay! It's lovely! Lovely!"

Her grandmother said casually, "It's ballet. *Les Sylphides*. But I'm sure you're far too young to want to watch it. It isn't for little girls."

"It's for *me*, though," Drina said. "Oh, Granny –!"

But, though she was in many ways very spoilt, it was never any use questioning her bedtime, and she found herself on her way upstairs.

"I'll come later and tuck you in," Mrs Chester said, from the sitting-room doorway.

Drina lingered at the top of the stairs to listen to the music, but after a few moments it was turned off and she heard her grandmother opening the drawers of her desk again.

She undressed and washed slowly, humming a few bars to herself and taking a dancing step or two with the sponge in her hand.

"Ballet!" she said to herself. "That's ballet. *Les Sylph* – something."

It was the first time she had ever heard the word 'ballet' and she was not to hear it much again for a very long time. Not until she was just ten and starting at a new school.

Drina knew Elleray School well. It was only a few hundred yards past her present school: a large, redbrick building in pleasant grounds, with a playing-field at the side. The girls wore a dark green uniform with a silver badge.

Drina was glad to go to Elleray, for she was finding the small and somewhat sedate school she attended rather boring. She was already one of the oldest amongst the boys and girls and she had no special friend there, though she was popular enough. It would be exciting, though perhaps rather alarming, to go to a bigger school, where there were girls much older than herself.

But first came the holidays, when she went with both her grandparents to the West of Scotland. Soon after their return, however, came the business of buying the new uniform, and she seemed to need a great many things – a dark green coat for winter days, a green skirt and jacket, several pale yellow blouses, and all sorts of shoes, including shoes for dancing.

Drina pricked up her ears at the mention of the dancing shoes.

"What kind of dancing will it be?"

"Oh, I believe they do English and Scottish folk dancing, and some National and Greek," Mrs Chester explained, with her head bent as she measured the hem of the new green skirt. She had decided that it was rather too long for Drina, who was so small and thin for her age.

"Oh!" Drina said, staring down at her grandmother's well arranged grey hair. She had not thought about dancing much for a very long time, though occasionally, when she was listening to music, the urge to move to it had been too strong for her. It seemed to be something that she just had to do. "And can *I* do it?"

"Of course. It's part of the ordinary curriculum. All

the girls dance."

"Oh!" said Drina again, and when she was released from her grandmother's measuring she ran upstairs and whirled and twirled before the long mirror on the landing. Then she paused and stared at herself rather disparagingly, finding nothing that she liked much about her heavy black hair, which was cut into a page boy curve just above her shoulders. Her eyes, wide and dark, were very large, and she was deeply sun-tanned after three weeks on the lovely, seaswept coast of Western Scotland. Her pink cotton dress was very short and her knees looked to her bony and rather silly.

"Not beautiful! Not even pretty!" she said aloud, though she was not usually given to thinking much about her appearance. "Plain and skinny!"

Two weeks later Drina awoke with a slight feeling of uneasiness and realised that it was the day her life would change. The new school suddenly loomed up before her, and she felt shy and rather inclined to shrink from facing a hundred and fifty strange girls and the possibly critical eyes and minds of the staff. Still, it had to be coped with and Drina was not lacking in courage. So she put on the new uniform and made a real attempt to eat a good breakfast.

It was a bright September morning and her heart lifted as she said goodbye to her grandmother and set off along the tree-lined roads of the suburb where she lived. She forced her mind away from school and instead looked with delight at the milky blue sky, the light on leaves just starting to turn gold here and there, the Michaelmas daisies and brilliant, heavy-headed dahlias in gardens. For the first time she could really smell autumn in the air and the distant factory chimneys were made almost ethereal by the faint blue mist.

She walked along briskly, swinging her school-bag, but when, after ten minutes or so, she saw the school buildings in front of her, she slackened her pace slightly. Girls in the same green uniform flashed past her on bicycles, several stepped, laughing, off a bus just ahead, and others were walking up a side road.

The worst began to happen. Drina was enveloped in shyness and would have given almost anything to be going as usual to the comfortable familiarity of the old school. She wished heartily that she had accepted her grandmother's offer to accompany her that first time, though it had not seemed necessary when the suggestion was made. After all, she had been with her to see the headmistress two days before and had seen over the school then. There was nothing to do now but to walk up the drive and round to the entrance. The cloakrooms were just inside the door and then, once her outdoor clothes were off and her shoes changed, she would only have to follow the crowd.

Drina, in company with many only and rather solitary children, had long ago developed the habit of talking to herself.

"*Do* have some courage!" she told herself fiercely. "You're almost ten. That's far too old to be taken to school like a baby!"

But she walked more and more slowly and, just within the school gate, came to a dead stop. She was still standing there, surveying the building, when someone cannoned into her and she staggered at the impact.

"Oh, sorry!" cried a breathless voice, and she found herself looking into a friendly, rosy face. "Didn't mean to batter you! But I always like to be early first day, and one of my idiot brothers had hidden my school-bag. They're always doing things like that. Hey, you must be new?"

"Yes," said Drina, at once feeling better. She immediately liked the fair hair, blue eyes and plump body of the other girl.

"Well, I'm not. I'm ten and I've been here for two terms. I'm Jenny Pilgrim. Walk with me and tell me your name. You don't want to go on standing here?"

"No. It was just that I was scared," Drina confessed. "I'm Andrina Adams. At least, it's Adamo, really, but Granny wants me to be called Adams. She likes it better."

"Andrina Adamo! How strange!" said Jenny, savouring the name with evident pleasure. "Much more romantic than plain Jenny Pilgrim!"

"But I'm nearly always called Drina. Except when anyone's mad with me, and they aren't very often."

Jenny gave a sympathetic giggle.

"I'm Jennifer when that happens, and people are often mad with me. I'm lazy and I do the silliest things sometimes. I'm not a bit what Mother expected, I'm afraid."

"Goodness! Why?" Drina was so intrigued with her new friend that she forgot to mind that they were approaching the side door.

"Oh, well, I'm the only girl and she rather wants me to like things I don't like. Why are you Adamo, really? Is it foreign?"

"Yes. My father was Italian. He's dead," Drina explained.

"Is he? I've got all my parents. Haven't you got a mother, either?"

"No. She's dead, too. I can't remember either of them. My father died when I was only a few months old, and my mother died before I was two, I think. But

I've got Granny and Grandfather, so I don't really mind."

"Fancy having an Italian father!" said Jenny, impressed. "Did your mother meet him in Italy?"

"I don't think so. He was a businessman from Milan, but he was often in London. Granny and Grandfather – and Mother, too, I suppose – lived in London once. They only came here when they took me to live with them. Grandfather got moved by his firm, I think, but they hardly ever talk about it," Drina explained rapidly. They were going through the door now and the cloakrooms were crowded with girls, all chattering very loudly.

Jenny pushed her way unconcernedly amongst them.

"Hullo, everyone! Don't say you've taken my peg, Polly? Well, never mind, I'll have this one, and Drina can be next to me. She's new. Hey!" she added under cover of the noise, as she changed her shoes. "What class are you in?"

"1A, Miss Morrison said."

"Good! So am I, at present, but I may be moved up into 2 before the end of the year. I should have gone up into 2 this term, but my report was awful. Anyway, it'll be nice to be together. My friends have all gone up. Could we," and she put her head on one side and smiled widely at Drina, "be friends, do you think? Or is it rather early to say?"

"I don't know. I think it would be fun," Drina said, a little shyly, but with greatly increased happiness. Life at the new school would be much easier with a ready made friend.

"Yes, it would! And we'll have lots of time to get to know each other. We'll have to find out the sort of things we like and don't like. I'd better warn you here and now that I spend a lot of my spare time dancing." Jenny said it as though it were something of which to be ashamed.

"Dancing?" Drina asked sharply. "How do you mean? Granny said that I'd learn dancing here, but –"

Jenny flicked her hair.

"Oh, not that kind. I don't mind dancing *Dashing White Sergeant* or those nice polka-y dances from Austria and Scandinavia and places. I do those quite well and it's fun. No, I mean serious dancing."

"Ballet?" Drina asked tentatively, and just then a bell made her jump.

"Yes, ballet. It's a dreadful bore, but Mother's so keen for me to be good. And how can I be when I'm so round? I just haven't got the figure for it! Look here! We'll have to go or we'll be last in the Hall and the prefects will glare."

"But I want to know –" Drina scarcely knew why it was so important.

"Well, tell you later. We'll have time to talk in Break. Shhh now. We're not allowed to talk in the main corridors. This place is full of 'Don'ts'." And Jenny led the way into the hall.

# 2

# Jenny Talks of Ballet

When the time for Break came at last, Jenny Pilgrim was as good as her word. She seized two bottles of milk and two straws and led Drina into a corner.

"We have to drink our milk fairly quickly and go out when it's fine. I'll show you the playing-field in a minute, but let's start talking now. You start! Where did you go for your holiday?"

"To Applecross on the coast of Wester Ross," Drina said, readily enough. "It was lovely. Gorgeous sea, and rocks and islands, and people with singing sorts of voices. Grandfather fished and Granny and I went for walks and bathed, and out in little boats. She's not so dreadfully old really, though her hair's grey –"

"I shall have to meet her, shan't I, if we're going to be friends? And you must come home with me. But were you with her all the time? Were there any other young people?"

"Not most of the time. There was another girl there when we arrived and I bathed with her a few times. I didn't really mind," Drina said. "I like the country a lot –"

Jenny's rosy face flushed a little more.

"So do I. I wish I could be in it all the time. Mother's sister is married to a farmer and they live out towards

Stratford-on-Avon. The farm's lovely: built of old red brick and half-timbering. I stayed there for a month, and I cleaned out the hens and the pigs and sometimes milked. I wished," and she gave a gusty sigh, "that I could be a farmer when I grow up."

"Well, p'rhaps you can. It'll be a long time before you grow up."

"I'll be one if I have anything to do with it, and I'm sure Madame thinks its the only thing I'll ever be able to do. *She* knows I'll never be a dancer, not even in the back row of the chorus, let alone in the corps de ballet in a real ballet company."

"I want to know about ballet," Drina said earnestly, quite forgetting the shyness she might normally have felt with a very new friend.

"All right, but if you've finished your milk we'd better go out and draw a few breaths of fresh air. They're horribly keen on air here; that's why every window in the classroom was open. It suits me, anyway, though some of the stuffies grumble." As they went along the corridor towards the side door Jenny added, "Though why you want to know about ballet I can't really imagine. Wouldn't you rather hear about the farm? I had to leave after a month because Mother said I'd only practise if I was at home, and now I'm back at the Dancing School three times a week."

"I'd *really* sooner hear about dancing, if you don't mind," Drina insisted.

Jenny surveyed her with bright, intelligent eyes. She might be lazy in class, but it was evident that she was not a stupid person.

"Don't tell me you're *another* ballet fan? Balletomane is the right word, of course," she said, rather grandly.

Drina, who had never heard the word, looked puzzled.

"No. I'm not a fan *or* a ballet – what you said. I don't know anything about it, but I want to."

"Now I come to think about it you *look* like a dancer. Ten times more so than me or half those idiots at the Selswick School who think about nothing but being ballerinas some day. A lot of hope they've got, too," she said scornfully. "They don't take a bit of notice of what Madame says, though she can be dreadfully scathing. I just curl up sometimes, and it's not *my* fault that I'm hopeless, but still keep on. She's always pointing out that only one in several thousand has a chance of being a ballerina, and one in a million a *prima ballerina assoluta.*"

The unfamiliar terms meant little to Drina, but she found herself glowing inwardly at the careless words, "You *look* like a dancer."

"But why do you have to learn dancing if you don't like it and aren't very good?" she demanded.

"Oh, because Mother's so keen. My mother isn't at all a silly sort of person over most things, but she made up her mind when I was little that I would dance. She rather wanted to herself when she was young, but never got the chance, and she vowed that her one daughter should manage it instead. There are five boys as well as me, and I wish I'd been a boy too. Of course, men *do* dance, but she might not have though of that," Jenny said rapidly. "She keeps on hoping that I'll improve, because, of course, I'm very young yet. I do try, but it's really hopeless. I don't think I shall ever get out of the beginners' class. I'm Madame's despair, though I think she rather likes me apart from that. I'm not so bad at mime; in fact, I rather like that. But I've still got to bear two ballet classes a week to one of mime."

"But where do you learn? Who is Madame?" Jenny

was going altogether too fast for Drina, who was already rather muddled after half a morning in a strange school.

"I go to the Janetta Selswick School of Dancing down in the town. Mother says it's a first class place; not like most of the Dancing Schools in the provinces," Jenny said glibly. "Miss Selswick is Madame, though she's not foreign like most of the teachers in all those idiotic stories about the ballet. She doesn't say, 'Ah, ze leetle one ees going to be ze dancer most pair-fect!' or 'Er I can do zomethink wiz *eef* she will work!'"

It was evident by her comical expression and the sudden effect of being a plumpish little foreign woman that Jenny might indeed be good in the mime class and Drina broke into delighted giggles.

"I've never read a ballet story. Are people really like that?"

"Never read a ballet story? I've got dozens. Mother buys them for me every birthday and Christmas, though luckily I get lots of book tokens, too, and can buy farming ones for myself. They're always about girls who want to be ballerinas and who manage it with no effort at all. Madame says she wishes someone would write one when it's made as hard as possible for the heroine and then the poor kid doesn't succeed in the end. But look here! If you're so keen why don't you learn dancing? If you like I'll give you the prospectus to show to your grandmother. Madame really was a ballerina with the Royal Ballet Company once. Mother used to go and watch her at Covent Garden when she was young. Mother lived in London and spent most of her money on theatre tickets. She never missed a new ballet, more's the pity! Come home for a little while after school and I'll find the prospectus for you."

Whole new worlds were opening for Drina, though she hadn't the faintest idea what Jenny meant by "the Royal Ballet" and "Covent Garden". Her face was unusually flushed and her heart was bumping with excitement.

"I don't know – I've always wanted to learn dancing. Ever since I was little. But I don't think – I don't think that Granny approves of it."

"Wow!" Jenny stared. "I wish Mother didn't! But why doesn't she approve? Does she think it wicked? Some people do. There's a girl in Class 2 whose parents are awfully religious in a stuffy sort of way and they really think dancing wicked. Not folk dancing, but ballroom and ballet. She feels rather bad about it."

For almost the first time, Drina really tried to define her grandmother's attitude and failed.

"I don't know. She's never *said* it's wicked. She doesn't say things like that. And how could it be anyway? Beautiful things are never wicked, are they? It's just that – just that she doesn't seem to like it. When I was very little she found me making a dance. I can just remember. There was lovely music on the radio and I was being a leaf in a dark wood, and she looked all funny. She nearly always does look a bit funny when I start to dance, and I did once ask to learn and she said I wasn't strong enough."

Jenny surveyed her with increased interest. "You're thin, but you look very healthy really."

"I'm sure I am now. I never need the doctor."

"Well – oh, bother! There's the bell. We'll have to fly. There won't be time at dinner-time, but after school this afternoon you come home with me and I'll lend you one of those silly ballet stories and find the prospectus. You can ask your grandmother, anyway."

"Oh, thank you!" Drina gasped and raced at Jenny's heels back into the school.

Her mind was so filled with thoughts of dancing that she paid little attention to the geography lesson that followed, but, as she was new, her class teacher, Miss Rigby, left her alone.

Jenny accompanied her some of the way home and them turned off up a side road. "Sometimes I cycle.

Have you got a bike?"

"Yes, but Granny said the walk would do me more good. We often go out into the country."

"We'll cycle together then sometimes. Mother doesn't mind my going because she knows I'm careful. Tell your grandmother you're coming home with me after school; then she won't worry."

Drina duly explained about visiting Jenny, but made no mention of ballet stories and the Selswick School prospectus. She looked so bright and pink-cheeked that Mrs Chester felt sure the new school was going to be a success and was pleased to hear about her friendship with Jenny Pilgrim.

Mr Chester, who had come home for lunch as he occasionally did, repeated the name with interest.

"Pilgrim? It's not a very usual name. Ask her if her father is one of the directors of Pilgrim, Watkin and Moore. We sometimes do business with them and Pilgrim is a very nice fellow. I've never met his family, but I should think his daughter might be a good friend for you. You must ask her here sometime."

"But don't rush into things," said Mrs Chester with some caution. "I do rather distrust sudden friendships, though she sounds a pleasant girl."

Drina returned to school extremely cheerfully and enjoyed the afternoon, especially as it included a dancing period. Class 1A was to concentrate on Scottish dancing that term and Drina, tense with eagerness, lined up with the others to practise the setting and Strathspey and reel steps. She had natural poise and a quick ear for music and after ten minutes or so, the teacher, a Miss MacDonnell, called her out.

"Have you done some Scottish dancing before?"

Drina shook her head till her black hair flew out. "Oh, no. I've never learned any sort of dancing."

"Well, you seem to have taken to it very quickly. That setting was really very good. Now, girls!" And she raised her voice. "Take partners and we'll start with *Petronella*. Some of you did it last term, remember?"

"Be my partner!" Jenny cried, grabbing Drina's hand.

Drina enjoyed every moment of the period, though she was mildly astonished at the muddle several of the sets got in. Miss MacDonnell's instructions seemed to her so clear and easy to follow and Jenny was a good partner.

"There!" Jenny said, as they dispersed. "That was quite fun, though nothing but a romp. In fact, I like romps best. It's a terrific feeling to be one of the best instead of a poor heavy idiot working at the *barre*."

"I liked it!" said Drina. "I liked it better than anything I've ever done. But – ballet's quite different, isn't it?"

"Of course it is. You'll soon see if you come to the Selswick School. Now just a French period and we can go home."

At four o'clock, Drina accompanied Jenny rather shyly homewards and within a quarter of an hour they were approaching a fairly large redbrick house in Elmwood Road.

"Have your people got lots of money?" Jenny asked.

Drina hesitated. It was something she had never thought about.

"I don't know. Our house is smaller than this, but – but Granny never says we haven't any money. And she did say not very long ago that I might go to boarding-school when I'm about fourteen. That costs a lot, doesn't it?"

"I should think it must. We're not badly off, but we'll all need training and Philip wants to be a doctor. *That* takes ages before they earn, you know."

Drina remembered then to ask if her father was the man her grandfather knew, and Jenny said that he must be.

"He *is* Pilgrim, Watkin and Moore. Fancy your grandfather knowing him! Well, that makes things a lot easier. Mother says it's vulgar to talk about money, but I don't really see why we shouldn't, do you? It's really interesting, after all, though just at the moment I only have my pocket money, and I won't earn much when I'm old enough to start farming I suppose. There'd certainly be more money in dancing. Perhaps you've got some of your own, you know. Your father may have left you some."

"I don't know," said Drina slowly, but it was a new idea.

Jenny led her into a big, pleasant sitting-room, where a fair-haired woman was starting to lay the tea table. She greeted Drina very kindly and was interested to learn that her husband and Drina's grandfather knew each other.

"And Drina wants to learn dancing, so I said I'd lend her the prospectus for the Selswick School," Jenny put in hastily.

Mrs Pilgrim groped amongst some papers on a side table.

"I always keep one by me in case anyone is interested. Here it is! Perhaps if Drina's keen she may make you work a bit harder. I suppose Jenny's told you that she wants to work on the land when she's older?" she asked, rather ruefully.

Drina flushed a little, feeling shy, but Jenny said cheerfully, "Of course I have. And I do work really, Mother. Madame sees to that. But I haven't a scrap of talent for ballet. Can you *see* me doing *fouettés* and *pirouettes*?"

"I hope to, one day," retorted Mrs Pilgrim. "You haven't given yourself a chance yet, Jenny. After all, ten is still very young, and if you didn't eat so many cakes and sweets you'd soon be less plump. Though when I spoke to Madame about that, she said you probably needed sugar and not to cut you down too much."

"I *like* cakes and sweets," said Jenny, grinning. "Here! Take the prospectus, Drina, and come and see my room."

"Will you stay to tea, dear?" Mrs Pilgrim asked, as they made for the door.

Drina hesitated. So far there was no sign of the boys, but she supposed that they would all be home soon and the knowledge made her shyer than ever.

"I don't think I'd better today, thank you," she said. "Granny's expecting me back."

"Well, another day. I'll give Jenny a note for your grandmother."

Jenny's room was a very small one over the front door, but it had attractive, if rather shabby, furniture and a great many pictures and photographs. Over the bookcase was a little country scene, with evening sunlight slanting across a cornfield. Jenny gazed at it with affection.

"Don't you love the poppies? I bought that picture myself with some of my birthday money."

But Drina had gone straight to a large photograph that showed Jenny poised on one foot with her arms outstretched. She wore a very brief, feathery costume and a little cap with two long feathers.

"Oh, that!" said Jenny, dismissing it. "I was a bird in our Summer Show at the Selswick, you know. A really plump bird that scarcely danced a step!"

"I think you look nice," said Drina gravely, still studying it.

"Well, I can just see *you* in tights and a tutu, with your hair tied back. Would you like to put mine on and see what you look like?"

"I don't know what a tutu is, but I'd love to. Only not now," said Drina prudently. Her grandmother did not like her to be late for meals and, during term-time, Drina was always provided with a high tea at five o'clock.

"Then choose a ballet book. Look at the rows of them! This is the first of a series — they're not bad, I must admit. And this is the most sensible one."

Drina took "the most sensible one", which had a picture of a girl in a white ballet dress on the jacket, and stowed it and the Selswick School prospectus in her school-bag. Then, rather reluctantly, she said goodbye and was soon hurrying towards her home.

As she went, she thought what a long day it had seemed and was surprised at how many new things she had learned. As for the prospectus, she found that she was not sure if she would have the courage to show it to her grandmother. Almost certainly, she would not be allowed to have dancing lessons, especially if she rushed things. It might be better to wait a while.

So when she reached home, she went upstairs with her school-bag, and the ballet story and the prospectus went into her middle drawer, beneath her clean underclothes and pyjamas.

"*Why* can't I tell her?" she asked herself, standing for a moment at the window and looking down at the bed of dark purple Michaelmas daisies in the garden below. "It seems mean and not honest, but — well, I won't yet, anyway. But somehow — *somehow* I'm going to dance!"

# 3

# The Watcher in the Ballet Class

**D**rina had never belonged to a public library and her books had all been carefully chosen for her by her grandmother. The ballet story, which she started that evening during the half-hour when she was allowed to read in bed, was a new experience and one so absorbing that she was reluctant to put it away when she heard her grandmother's footsteps on the stairs. Somehow she immediately felt at home in the world of ballet school and theatre, which was curious, as she had only been inside a theatre a few times in her life.

At Christmas she was usually taken to the pantomime at the Grand Theatre in Willerbury, and occasionally in between she had been to a musical, if it was thought suitable. Only once had she been to a London theatre and that had been to a Gilbert and Sullivan opera, *The Yeoman of the Guard*, which she had found rather boring.

Yet she felt a definite kinship with the boys and girls who got jobs in the theatre when they were only twelve, and she really suffered at having to put away the book when the heroine, Perdita, having failed to get a job with the others, worked alone at the *barre* in the practice room at the ballet school.

She felt almost guilty when her grandmother kissed

her goodnight, and it was only that feeling of guilt that prevented her from switching on the light again and going on with the story. Poor, poor Perdita, who was really one of the best dancers, but who was poor and shy and at times so awkward that Madame – very foreign, with a terrific accent – was often angry with her.

Drina slept at last and dreamed that, clad only in a feathery cap, she was dancing in a wintry wood. The extreme cold of the wood awoke her, and she found that half the bedclothes were on the floor and the first light was creeping through the partly closed curtains.

She had little chance to speak to Jenny before school, but at Break her new friend captured her and, over bottles of milk, demanded, "Well, how do you like Perdita? And what did your grandmother say about the Selswick?"

Drina flushed.

"I love Perdita, though that foreign Madame made me laugh. I kept on seeing *you*! But I – I haven't shown Granny the prospectus."

"Why on earth not?"

"I – I don't know. I thought I'd wait. I – I don't somehow think she'll like it."

Jenny looked at her with a shrewdness that would not have disgraced someone much older.

"I don't know why you should be scared."

"I don't know either. But I am a bit. And yet Granny's always kind. She's a dear and I love her, but – but I don't always understand her."

"I should think you're imagining it about the dancing. But keep the pros. for a bit, if you like. Shall *I* ask her for you?"

"Oh, don't!" cried Drina, in a panic. "I mean – no, I'll ask her soon. But not yet. I – I haven't even told her about your dancing."

"Well, it seems really strange, but perhaps you know best. Still, I should think she'll *have* to let you dance in the end. You're made for it."

"You can't know," said Drina, flushing more deeply than ever.

"No, perhaps I can't. And yet I've seen all sorts of dancers since I went to the Selswick, and, you know, I'm really interested in people. I watch them a lot, when I ought to be thinking about steps and getting my arms right. I just feel it in my bones that you'd be good, and you know what Miss MacDonnell said yesterday? She only knows about Scottish, of course, but you *were* quick. Lots of them will take all term to learn to set and even then they'll mess up *Petronella*."

"I want to dance. I *will* ask her. But not yet," Drina said, and then she strove very hard to put all thoughts of dancing out of her mind, a very necessary resolution, for the teaching at Elleray School was good and the standard of work high. She would only be in trouble if she sent in badly written exercises and did not know what had been said in class.

So she settled down to work and, after two or three days, felt quite happy at school. She liked Jenny more and more, but there were other nice girls, too, who seemed ready to be friendly. It was certainly a great improvement on her former school and Drina was never bored for a moment. She had far too much to cope with.

The weekend was a quiet time, but it gave her a chance to finish the story of Perdita, and Jenny had thoughtfully provided a second book, the first in a long series. On the Sunday morning, Drina went to church with her grandmother, and in the afternoon, Mr Chester took them out into the country in the car.

The lovely Warwickshire countryside looked beautiful under the September sun, and when they passed an attractive farmhouse built in mellow old red brick, Drina thought of Jenny and wondered if it could possibly be her uncle's farm. But there were many like it, and delightful little cottages, with gardens simply bursting with autumn flowers and apples still glowing on the trees.

They had tea in Stratford, at a hotel by the river and, looking towards the great Memorial Theatre, Mr Chester said suddenly, "We ought to bring Drina here next summer. She's surely quite old enough for Shakespeare? She'd probably love *A Midsummer Night's Dream*, if they were by any chance doing that."

"Oh, yes!" Drina cried, with a dim feeling that there might be dancing in *The Dream*, which they had had read to them during her last term at her old school. There were fairies, weren't there? And Puck? Anyway, it would be better than nothing and the huge theatre, standing so boldly by the Avon, had always attracted her.

On the way home, she realised with a little thrill of pleasure that the next morning she would see Jenny again and might hear more about the Selswick School.

And Jenny's first words were, "Look here! I've had an idea! I'm sure Madame wouldn't mind if you'd like to watch this afternoon. I have my ballet class at half-past four."

"Oh, surely I couldn't?" Drina asked, wide-eyed.

"I don't see why not. People often come to watch, and we can tell her that you're going to ask if you can join. She's really very nice when she isn't roaring that we're like sacks of flour and haven't a hope of getting on any stage at all, or even of becoming dancing teachers in some awful little school. Why don't you tell your grandmother that you'll be late and come with me?"

Drina was sorely tempted, but she was pretty sure that any such request would be refused. But fate played into her hands, for her grandmother said at lunch:

"I shall be home late this afternoon, Drina. I've got a meeting of the Ladies' Club at four-thirty. But Mrs Tring will have your tea all ready, and I shan't be later than six."

"Well, actually, will it matter if I'm late, too?" Drina asked. "Jenny wants me to go – she asked –"

Mrs Chester was in a hurry to make some telephone calls and was paying very little attention.

"Oh, well, if Jenny wants you to go home with her that will fit in very nicely and I needn't worry about your being lonely."

She rose soon after that and could be heard telephoning in the little lobby off the hall. Drina drew a long breath and began slowly to turn the pages of a magazine, without seeing a word. She felt very mean and guilty, for she was not used to deceiving her grandmother. And yet it couldn't be so dreadful a thing to go to the Selswick School with Jenny. Surely it couldn't? And she wanted to go more than she had ever wanted anything in her life.

But her conscience troubled her so much that when she was ready to go, with her school-bag in her hand, she went to see her grandmother. Mrs Chester had just finished a call and was about to make another one. She had lately begun to take a great interest in several clubs and her time was more occupied than formerly.

"Granny, I just wanted to tell you – Jenny's going to take me –"

Her grandmother gave her a hasty kiss and gentle

push in the direction of the front door.

"You're rather late, Drina, Do hurry, dear. You don't want to get any black marks or anything. Take care."

Drina gulped, hesitated, and then went. At least she had tried, and that made her feel rather better.

"I'm coming with you," she informed Jenny, as they got their books out for a history lesson.

Jenny grinned.

"Oh, good! Coming to see the lovely sacks of flour! I told you your grandmother wouldn't mind."

"I – I didn't tell her. I tried, but she was busy and wouldn't listen. She's going out to a meeting and will be back late. She thought I meant I was going home with you."

Jenny arranged her pencils carefully.

"Oh, well, that's all right. You can tell her afterwards. You'll have to, of course, if you're going to ask if you can have lessons."

"But –" Drina was beginning unhappily, when the door opened and the history teacher entered.

Drina had, however, more or less forgotten her troublesome conscience by the time that school was over and she and Jenny were waiting for the bus. Jenny carried a little case instead of her school-bag; it contained her practice clothes and shoes.

The bus came very soon and they were jolted quickly down into the town. In no more than seven minutes, they were darting up a side street and approaching a large, rather grim building that bore the words "Janetta Selswick School of Dancing". A smaller notice said, "Classes in ballet, mime, tap and ballroom dancing. All ages".

Once there, Drina began to feel shy and awkward and sure that she would be snubbed, but Jenny bore her quickly through the swing door and along a somewhat dark corridor. In the distance Drina could hear more than one piano and a voice from a nearby room was saying, "*One*, two, three. *One*, two, three. Rest!"

"That's just the ballroom class. You aren't interested in that," said Jenny and plunged down a flight of steep stairs and into a cloakroom, where girls of various ages were changing. Drina stood silently to one side while Jenny hastily dragged off her coat, skirt and blouse and began to put on her brief practice clothes. Then she pinned back her hair.

"It gets in the way. It's better pinned back."

The new style made a great difference to her face, and altogether she looked rather unfamiliar. Drina would have given anything at all to have been standing there in similar clothes, ready to *learn*.

"Come on! Madame can't bear anyone to be late," Jenny said briskly and led the way up the stairs again, along the corridor and up another flight of stairs. Drina followed, breathless, anxious and deeply fascinated already. A bunch of big girls in practice dress hurried past and one of them said, "So I told her that if I can't be principal dancer I think it's a shame, when –"

"Oh, that's Carol!" said Jenny. "She thinks herself the shining light of that amateur company that gives a pantomime at the Royal every Christmas: the Daffodils. She'll never be more than an amateur, either."

"You do know a lot," cried Drina, with genuine admiration, but Jenny went pink.

"I don't really. It's just what I hear Madame and the others say. But Carol's too lumpy, like me. Only she's got a ballet mother, too. Poor mother!"

Then they were in the doorway of a large, light studio and someone was playing odd snatches of ballet music on the piano. A few girls and three boys were doing exercises at the *barre*.

Drina hung back, feeling conspicuous in her school clothes, but Jenny said cheerfully, "You go and sit in the corner. I'll go and start, but I'll explain to Madame when she comes. She takes most of the ballet classes herself, you know."

Drina crept into the corner near the piano and watched more and more students arriving – lucky, lucky people who had the chance of learning ballet from Janetta Selswick, once a ballerina in the Royal Ballet Company. Drina now had a slight idea of what that meant, thanks to Jenny's well-informed chatter.

Some of the girls were as old as twelve or thirteen and others were very small, looking scarcely eight, though Jenny had also told her that it was harmful to start ballet training before eight and Madame was very much against taking such young pupils. About ten was the ideal age to sart.

There were thin girls and rather plump ones; ones that looked angular and awkward in their practice clothes and a very few who looked quite at ease, graceful and, in some cases, very pretty. The boys were fewer in number and mostly not older than ten or eleven.

Drina remembered that it was a beginners' class and wondered what the more advanced students would look like.

She was dreaming and staring, watching the exercises at the *barre*, when she suddenly realised that someone with iron grey hair and a body that was still beautiful and pliant had entered the room. The pianist leaped up to greet her and those at the *barre* immediately stopped what they were doing and said:

"Good afternoon, Madame!"

Jenny came forward without self-consciousness and

spoke quietly to Madame, who, after a few moments, turned towards Drina. Drina stood up, flushed and shy, but desperately eager, and Janetta Selswick gave her one quick, noticing glance.

"Well, my dear, Jenny tells me that you want to watch the class. Of course you may. Have you learned dancing?"

"Never. But I want to more than anything else in the world."

Janetta Selswick was used to hearing little girls say just that and she usually received the words with some reserve, but there was something about this girl with the dark eyes, the straight black hair and the good posture that struck her as unusual. The child had personality and intensity and she stood well.

"Drina wants to come here. She's going to ask her grandmother if she may," said Jenny.

"Then I hope that her grandmother will agree," said Janetta Selswick, who smiled and turned back to her class.

Drina sank down again, with a humming in her ears and her face very hot. And it was some time – almost ten minutes – before she gave her full attention to what was going on. Her thoughts had been far away, for she was wondering how she could get her heart's deisre. Then she began to watch the work at the *barre*, noticing, even in her complete lack of knowledge, that some, like Jenny, looked awkward and stiff and others much more pliant, with bodies that moved easily and gracefully. It was a revelation to her that so much attention had to be given even to standing correctly at the *barre*, but then she heard Madame explaining patiently to a worried-looking girl that to stand correctly was the basis of all ballet training. From that, all things might follow; without it, one was permanently handicapped.

Then the centre practice began and Drina watched even more intently, giving at least half her attention to Madame and the rest to the moving figures. Words that she had never heard rang in her ears: *plier*, *éntendre*, *glisser*. But yes, they were all French, of course, and *glisser*, at least, she knew. It meant to slide.

She watched as Jenny, flushed and anxious, tried again and asgain to achieve the correct movement and failed; and suffered with her when Madame, abandoning kindness and quiet speech, shouted that she would never dance – no, never! It was a waste of time and her parents' money to try and teach her.

But almost immediately, Madame's attention was given to a fair, rather smug girl, who had gone through the exercises with a fixed smile, obviously rather pleased with herself. She looked a good deal less smug a few minutes later.

It looked quite easy to Drina. She watched and noted and resolved to try some of the steps and movements in her room at home, or in the bathroom, where the towel-rail might perhaps be used as a *barre*. It was terribly hard to sit there, listening to the music and feeling too hot in her thick coat. She longed with her whole heart to be out there under Madame's all-seeing eyes, and when, at the end, the class was told to improvise to a piece of lovely, lilting ballet music it was all she could do not to fling off her coat and join them, outdoor shoes and all.

Jenny joined her in her corner when the class was over.

"Well, do you see why I'm hopeless? Madame thinks so, doesn't she? She actually told Mother that she didn't think she could make even a moderately good dancer of me. But Mother just smiled and said I'd only just started and there was time yet."

"Most of them love it," said Drina, as they went downstairs again at the back of the leaping, laughing crowd.

"Oh, well, half of them dream every night of being ballerinas. I'd sooner dream of pigsties." And Jenny gave a too loud laugh, pulled a face and snorted violently as a way of relieving her feelings.

"I wish, wish that I could come!"

"Well, don't be such an idiot! Ask your grandmother. She can't eat you, can she?"

"No," Drina agreed soberly, and that night, when she was sitting peacefully by the sitting-room fire with her grandmother, she did gather the courage to broach the subject. Mrs Chester listened, at first in bewilderment and then with the expression that Drina dreaded settling on her face. But she merely said:

"I didn't know that Jenny Pilgrim was so keen on dancing."

"She isn't. She wants to be a farmer. But her mother wants her to learn. Granny, please may I have lessons, too? Ballet lessons."

Mrs Chester was knitting very rapidly.

"I really think you've got enough to cope with, Drina dear, with a new school and quite a lot of homework. But if you really want to take up something new I suggest that you have piano lessons. You seem to love music, and it would not be nearly so tiring as dancing lessons after a hard day at school."

Drina sat pleating the hem of her skirt, her hair swinging forward to hide her face.

"I'd like to learn the piano, Granny. Jenny says that it's part of every dancer's training – learning music, you know. But –"

"Jenny says!" Mrs Chester repeated, with rare sharpness. "This Jenny seems to have talked a great deal."

"Yes, she's told me a lot. She doesn't want to dance, but her mother knows a lot about the ballet. She told me all about the Royal Ballet School, and the wonderful company that dances at Covent Garden in London and sometimes in New York and other places. And about the Igor Dominick School. They have their own company, too, and are as good as the Royal Ballet. One of the girls from the Selswick School got a scholarship there only last term, and –"

"You certainly seem to have picked up a lot," Mrs Chester said more quietly. "But it seems to me that a little girl of ten's thoughts would be better given over to school work and play."

"But, Granny, I would so like to go –"

"Well, wait a while, anyway. You couldn't start until

after Christmas, and by then I expect you'll have forgotten all about it. But we'll see about a good music teacher at once and get you started on that."

Drina said no more. She wanted to shout, to argue, to say that she *must* learn dancing. But, though she had had a temper as a very small child, it had been firmly repressed by her grandmother's sensible, kindly upbringing.

She drank her milk in silence and went slowly and droopingly up to bed. Hours later, it seemed, she heard voices in the passage; voices only just loud enough to be heard. Her grandmother was saying, "I wish she'd never made friends with that Pilgrim child. I wonder if it's too late to stop it?"

And her grandfather, calm, reasonable, "Surely that's not necessary, Claire? Drina's fond of Jenny already and she sounds a most sane and sensible child. And if what Drina says is true she's more interested in farms than in dancing. Besides, I certainly don't want to do anything to upset Pilgrim. After all, he's a business acquaintance, and –"

Mrs Chester made a sound like "Tssch!", but added, "Well, I hope we won't hear any more about ballet."

"Perhaps it's unavoidable, and it won't hurt the child to have a few lessons –"

Then a door shut and the house was quite silent. Drina lay staring rigidly into the darkness, with a mixture of fright and hope in her heart. Surely they wouldn't stop her friendship with Jenny? It had really sounded as though her grandfather would be opposed to that, and he could be firm when he wished. And after all, he had said –

"I won't give up. I'll ask again. I don't understand, but I mean to learn dancing." Then she turned over and fell asleep again.

# 4

# At the Grand Theatre

Mrs Chester was as good as her word and a music teacher was duly found for Drina. She was to come to the house in Beech Road once a week, and Drina thoroughly enjoyed the first lesson, not finding the work in the least wearisome. She genuinely wanted to be able to play the piano, to make her own music, and at the back of her mind was the thought that it would help her dancing when the time came, as surely it would.

Jenny was puzzled and rather indignant to hear that the dancing lessons had been refused, but she was interested to learn about the music.

"It'll be a help. Madame always says that. I learn, too, of course, but I'm not much better at that than I am at ballet. Dear me! I don't know why poor helpless girls should be forced into things that don't suit them. What I'd *like* to do is milk twice a week instead of leaping about like a lamb in spring! I'm going to ask my aunt to talk to Mother. *She* knows I'm the country type and not cut out to be any kind of dancer."

"It's really strange," said Drina, who had been thinking a good deal lately. "You can have dancing and I can't. Oh, and I've finished the third book in that series. Can I have the next?"

"All of them," said Jenny generously. "But don't run away with the idea that it's as easy as that."

"I won't. I know it's hard. Years of hard work. I shouldn't mind a bit, either.

"I don't believe you would. Anyhow, your grandmother did say she'd think about it again."

"Yes, but I don't believe she meant it. I wonder if I could tackle Grandfather? But he usually agrees with what she says – on the surface, anyway."

"Well, leave it for a little. You're only just ten. There's no dreadful hurry."

But to Drina there was need for haste, though she resolutely stifled her longing and really worked as hard as possible at school. She enjoyed most of the lessons, disliked games intensely, though she was light and quick, and looked forward to the two dancing periods. They were always too short, unlike the netball periods, which sometimes seemed to last for an eternity, especially on days when the ground was muddy and a cold wind made her eyes smart.

A fortnight passed and then one morning, Jenny arrived in the cloakroom with a rush, two minutes before the bell was due to ring.

"I've got a note from Mother to your grandmother. I suppose you'll be thrilled, though it's only a third-rate company, Mother says."

"What is?" asked Drina, hastily running a comb through her straight hair. It was a windy morning and she was not very tidy. "What do you mean?"

"There's a Ballet Company coming to the Grand Theatre next week. The British Ballet Company, they call themselves. Mother says they'll probably be very bad, but she thinks it's better than nothing. She always wishes I could see more ballet. She's got three seats in the front of the circle and she wants you to come with us."

The bell rang then, but Drina scarcely heeded it.

"Me! To see real ballet? Oh, Jenny!"

Jenny seized her firmly by the arm and propelled her towards the hall.

"Well, it's nice to feel that someone's pleased. There's a gorgeous Western on at the Odeon cinema next week and I'd ten times sooner go to that. I shall, too, on Saturday afternoon, if my pocket money runs to it. We're going to the ballet on Friday night. Mother doesn't like matinées and she says it won't hurt us to be a bit late at the end of the week. Anyway, it starts at seven and will be over by half-past nine, and she'll run you home in the car. The note's in my school-bag. Remind me to give it to you."

Drina took the note home with her, but said nothing about the invitation at lunch-time, when her grandfather was not present. She felt that it would be best to wait until he was there.

So she produced it that evening, when she had done her homework and the three of them were sitting by the fire. Her grandmother read the note with a slight frown and then passed it to her husband, while Drina waited in breathless anxiety, her hands clasped so tightly round her knees that the bone showed through her thin flesh.

"It's really very kind of Mrs Pilgrim, but I hardly think –" Mrs Chester began.

"Oh, Granny!" Drina cried, in an agony of despair.

"I don't approve of your going out late during the school term, as you know. You're very pale now that the holiday tan has worn off and you seem to work hard at school. I shall write to Mrs Pilgrim and thank her, but say –"

"Well, now, Drina hasn't been anywhere much since the beginning of term, and it would be an experience for her," Mr Chester said slowly, looking up from the note. "After all, it's poor reward for all her hard work at school if we just say that she must go to bed early every night."

"An experience that she can easily do without, and children shouldn't expect rewards for school work. It's only a third-rate company, anyway, and –"

"Mrs Pilgrim said that," said Drina, with a faint gasp. "How did *you* know, Granny?"

Mrs Chester flushed, but said mildly, "My dear Drina, I'm not entirely uninformed. This company is new and not particularly promising, by what I've read. And you're far too young to understand a ballet like *Giselle*, even though they're only doing the second act. Also *Les Sylphides* and *Le Spectre de la Rose*, according to Mrs Pilgrim's note."

Drina was deeply astonished. She had not expected her grandmother to know anything about ballets.

"Oh, Granny, I didn't know you'd seen ballet! But I'm not too young. I've heard about *Le Spectre de la Rose*. Jenny told me. She saw it once. The male dancer leaps through the window, and –"

Her grandmother looked at her with rather a strange expression.

"Don't be ridiculous, Drina! Why should I not have seen ballet?"

"But you – you never talk about it, and –"

"I think we'll have to let Drina go," said Mr Chester, in his firmest voice. "If she's bored, that's her lookout, after all. And we can hardly refuse when Mrs Pilgrim has so kindly bought an extra ticket, and in the circle, too, which is always the most expensive for ballet."

To Drina's intense relief her grandmother gave way

with a good grace, though her brow was still creased.

"Very well, I'll write and accept. But remember, Drina, there are to be no more late outings until Christmas."

"I'll remember. Oh, thank you, Granny!" And Drina enveloped her in a wild hug.

Mrs Chester disengaged herself gently and straightened her immaculate hair.

"All right. It's settled and there's no need to get so worked up. It must be your Italian blood."

Drina was startled, as her father was very rarely mentioned.

"Must it? Jenny would say that that was romantic."

"There's nothing especially romantic about Italians. Your father was mostly an extremely sensible man – a good businessman and highly intelligent. But he was at times rather more excitable than English people. Now run and get your milk, Drina dear. It's nearly time for bed."

And Drina, trailing off to the kitchen, thought that most interesting conversations seemed to end with the threat of bed. It was most frustrating, but at least she had learned a little more about her father. She had only one photograph of him: a portrait that showed him as very dark and handsome. Of her mother she had three, and she looked at them often with great curiosity, though they were not very clear. Betsy Chester (Adamo, of course, after her marriage) had had chestnut hair, arched eyebrows and rather a wide, smiling mouth. Drina had often wished that there were more photographs, especially when her mother was older, but her grandmother had never produced others. She had once said that they had been lost during the move from London and had not seemed to want to discuss the matter further. Drina had decided that it must be because her mother was dead and her grandmother still minded about it.

The next morning she met Jenny on the way to school and imparted her news.

"I can come. And isn't it funny? Granny knows a bit about ballet!"

"Most people know *something*," Jenny said sagely. "Well, it's really great that you can come. I suppose she won't let you come to the Western, too?"

"I don't think I'd better ask. And, besides, I don't like Westerns much. There's always such a lot of shooting and riding."

"And wide open spaces!" said Jenny, smacking her lips. "Nothing narrow and – and confined like ballet."

"You are funny!" said Drina, giggling. She always found Jenny's remarks unusual and amusing. She didn't talk in the least like the other girls.

After that, Drina simply lived for the Friday night when she would go to the ballet. The posters were up all over the town and she rolled the names of the ballets on her tongue – *Le Spectre de la Rose, Swan Lake, Giselle, Divertissement.*

"What's *Divertissement*?" she asked Jenny.

"Oh, lots of little bits of dances. Not half so boring as a great long thing like *Swan Lake*. But Mother says she's glad there's no *Divertissement* on our night."

The names of the dancers were fascinating, too. The ballerina was called Joanelle Tenovitch and her name was in very large print.

"She's probably Joan Smith really," said Jenny cheerfully, refusing to be impressed.

Friday night came at last. Drina, so excited that she could hardly cope with zips and hair ribbons, put on her pretty red velvet dress. In the end, her grandmother had to tie the ribbon that held back her hair and was arranged in a flat bow on top of her head. The effect was very attractive and Jenny, when she rang the doorbell and was faced with Drina, was obviously impressed.

"You look fantastic! Put on your coat and come on. Mother's waiting in the car."

"Wouldn't she like to come in?" asked Mrs Chester, as Drina struggled into her best grey coat.

"No, thank you, Mrs Chester. She wants to park the car early. There's a show on at the Royal, too, and the car park always gets full," Jenny said rapidly. She seized Drina's hand and they ran down the path through the cold, dark air.

Drina felt as though she must be dreaming as they sped down into the well-lighted streets of the town. She was going to see a ballet company – her first ballet company! And she didn't care in the least if they *were* third-rate and if Joanelle Tenovitch's real name was Joan Smith.

"Anyway," said Jenny, almost as though she had read her thoughts, *"you'll* be all right if you're ever a dancer. Andrina Adamo! It sounds lovely, but everyone will think you've made it up "

The Grand Theatre was very large and very old-fashioned and it had a reputation for being cold, draughty and inconvenient. But to Drina, as she climbed the stairs to the Circle, it seemed quite perfect, almost like heaven. She looked round at the gilded pillars and at the fat cherubs above the curtain and drew a deep breath. Somehow it had never seemed such an exciting place during the pantomime, though she had usually enjoyed being there.

Their seats were the best in the house, in the very middle of the Dress Circle, and she settled down rapturously to look at the programme. Mrs Pilgrim had bought them one each, saying that she thought it a good idea to keep theatre programmes; then in later years, you always knew just what and whom you had seen. Drina resolved to put the ballet programme in her treasure box when she got home.

"You'd better read it carefully," Mrs Pilgrim said kindly, rather impressed by her intensity. Though she had fought hard for Jenny's interest, she was beginning to admit to herself that her own daughter's heart was not in dancing or anything to do with the theatre. "You'll see that it gives the story of each ballet. Well, not of *Les Sylphides*, of course. That hasn't any story."

Drina looked down at the words "*Les Sylphides*" and, under them, to the names of the dancers. The ballet was evidently split up into dances – Nocturne, Valse, Mazurka. Dimly she remembered graceful white figures moving on the television screen and Chopin's lovely music.

"*Les Sylphides!*" she said softly to herself. It had a lovely sound.

"Of course every ballet company dances it," Mrs Pilgrim explained. "But it can still be beautiful. Though I have my doubts about this company."

Drina, however, had no doubts at all as the lights dimmed and the music began to steal through the theatre. Softly the curtain rose, revealing the blue-lit stage and the grouped white-clad figures.

Immediately she was quite carried away into another world, a world of drifting movement, of white arms and changing music. Mrs Pilgrim, with her much greater knowledge, might see the points of technique that were by no means perfect; she might remember other dancing figures on a far bigger and more important stage. But for Drina, it was the first time, and the first time was a miracle of beauty.

When, after the Finale, the curtain went down and the lights revealed clapping figures with chocolate boxes on their knees, she blinked and sighed and looked so dazed that Mrs Pilgrim left her alone, speaking to Jenny on her other side.

Drina ate an ice cream, but without tasting it at all. She was only waiting for the curtain to go up again, to see what that one word "*Giselle*" might mean. The note in the programme was rather hard to understand and it seemed very sad that Giselle should lie in her grave in the forest glade.

"Of course, they're only doing the second act," Mrs Pilgrim explained. "And I always like the first act myself. It's very moving when Giselle goes mad and kills herself."

Drina might not quite understand the story, but she watched the ethereal Wilis, lost again in that magical world of movement and music, and during the second interval she came awake enough to remember that the dancers were real people. At that moment, probably,

they were drinking tea and chattering in the dressing-rooms behind the stage. They must once have been students at dancing schools, doing exercises at the *barre* and perhaps shrinking before some angry and scornful Madame.

It was during *Le Spectre de la Rose*, as the dreamy music changed to an increasing crescendo of leaping, airy sound, that Drina had the moment of sharp realisation and resolution. *She* was going to be a dancer. She had thought that she might, hoped that she might be, but suddenly there was not the slightest doubt. It seemed as sure as the fact that she would gradually grow up. And, of course, the first requirement was that she should go to the Selswick School and work hard in the beginners' ballet class.

In the face of that certainty, she could not doubt that her grandmother would agree, though almost at the same moment she had a quick vision of the controlled face, grey hair and brisk voice of the woman who had been a mother to her.

She came back to the stage with a jerk as the male dancer leaped through the window, and then, soon, it was all over. She was herself again, though rather stiff and dazed. Jenny, to Mrs Pilgrim's amusement and chagrin, was sound asleep.

"Well, did you ever! I wish I could think it was only because she didn't find them good enough. They should never have attempted *Le Spectre*. That male dancer certainly wasn't up to it."

"But I shan't sleep in the Western!" Jenny assured them, yawning as they went to the cloakroom to fetch their coats.

"It was lovely! Lovely!" Drina said, as they drove back to the quieter, darker suburbs. "Thank you *very* much, Mrs Pilgrim, for taking me. I shall never, never forget it!"

"I wish I could take you to Covent Garden," said Mrs Pilgrim, with a faint sigh. How unfair life was that other people's children wanted and were suitable for the thing that you desired for your own daughter! "In my time, I've seen all the great ones – including Ivory."

"Ivory!" Drina repeated. "What a lovely name!"

"She was Elizabeth Ivory, and in some ways the greatest of them all. You find her in all the ballet books. Not the stories that you're reading, of course, but in the history of the ballet. Her *Giselle* was something quite unforgettable, and she created many new roles, too. Well, here we are, and I expect your grandmother will be waiting for you. Goodnight, dear."

"Goodnight!" cried Drina and ran up the path to the front door. The light sprang up as she put out her hand to the bell and in a minute or two she was sitting by the fire, drinking her milk and finding herself suddenly wordless.

"It was lovely!" was all she could say in answer to her grandmother's enquiries.

"I suppose you were bored?" said Mrs Chester, almost as though she wanted to believe it.

Drina opened her eyes very wide and strove to cope with the real world.

"Oh, not bored. It was – I've never seen anything like it before."

"Well, you look worn out. I don't think it was a good idea. Off you go to bed and you must sleep late in the morning."

As she lay in bed, Drina made up her mind that she must choose her time and then tackle her grandmother. It had to be done and soon. Nothing, nothing should stop her having lessons from Madame at the Selswick School.

# 5

# Purely for Pleasure

All Saturday, Drina thought about dancing, and in the evening, in that propitious hour when they were all three together, she suddenly nerved herself to the point. She stood up on the rug, a slim little figure in a short blue dress.

"Granny, have I got any money of my own?"

Her grandmother immediately dropped her knitting and her grandfather put down *The Times*. She was startled by their faces, but went on bravely.

"*Have* I, please? Or do you pay for everything?"

Mrs Chester retrieved her knitting and, with her head still bent, said quietly, "What an extraordinary question, Drina! But yes, you have quite a lot of money."

"Did my father leave it to me?"

"Well, yes, he left you some, and – you will be quite well off when you're older. Why do you ask?"

"But can't it be used now? Must I wait a long time?"

"It can be used for your education, of course. In fact, we'll send you to boarding-school if you seem strong enough when you're about fourteen. I told you that before."

"But I am strong. I'm never ill now."

"Yes, you're much better than you were. Why? What

is all this?"

Drina faced them, desperately eager and anxious.

"Granny, if I've got money, can't it be used to give me ballet lessons? It just *must* be used, because I've got to learn right away. You said wait till Christmas, but truly I can't wait. I – I don't mean to be rude," as she saw their faces. "But –" And suddenly her repressed side awoke and took possession of her. "I mean to dance! I *must* dance! If you won't let me, you're cruel!"

"Calm yourself at once, Drina dear," Mrs Chester said, very quietly. "I really think you forget yourself. Have we ever been cruel to you?"

"No," Drina said, suddenly choky. "No, you've been dears, both of you. But I've *got to learn to dance*. I truly have. It's not a bit of good stopping me. I – I'll find some way! Grandfather –"

Mr Chester had forgotten all about *The Times*. He was looking very grave.

"Drina, you run away and let us discuss this. Your grandmother has only been thinking of you. She thinks you have enough to do."

Drina ran and took refuge in the little lobby, which was very cold and draughty. It was quite ten minutes before they called her back and then everything seemed normal again. Her grandfather even handed her a chocolate, which she ate because she did not know what else to do with it. It was he who spoke.

"We've decided that if you feel like that you must have dancing lessons. But wouldn't ballroom or perhaps Greek or tap do? They wouldn't be quite such hard work."

A great weight seemed to roll off Drina's heart.

"Oh, thank you! No, not ballroom or tap. It must be ballet with Madame at the Selswick School. She's really good. She once danced with the Royal Ballet, you know. And may I start at half-term, please, if she'll take me? I just can't wait till after Christmas."

"Oh, I suppose so," said her grandmother. "I'll take you down to see this Madame on Monday afternoon after school."

"She – she has the beginners' class at half-past four. Could we get there before that? Or we could watch the class."

"I hardly think that will be necessary. I'll ring up and make an appointment for about ten past. I can give you a note to your teacher, asking her to let you out ten minutes early. And now you'd better do something to calm yourself before you go to bed. Fetch that new jigsaw and we'll do it together."

Drina wanted to leap and sing, but she obediently fetched the jigsaw and tried to give her mind to sorting the pieces of blue sky.

She was going to join the Selswick School!

"Oh, may I telephone Jenny?" she pleaded, as the last piece went into place.

"She may be in bed. Won't it wait till tomorrow? You could go round there in the afternoon."

"Oh, but I want to tell her now, please." And Drina, scenting permission, rushed back to the lobby, which no longer seemed cold, and dialled the Pilgrims' number. Jenny herself answered, and she listened to the news with gratifying interest.

"Good for you, Drina! I knew you'd manage it. Well, that's one person happy, anyhow!"

"Oh, I wish you were happy, too!" Drina gasped.

"Oh, I'm all right. I'm going to the farm for half-term. Mother will be pleased that you're going to the Selswick. Last night, when you'd left us, she said, 'That's one girl who cares about ballet!'"

"We're going to see Madame on Monday!" Drina

cried, and she sang loudly all the time she was washing and undressing. Then, in her pyjamas, she suddenly grew more sober and, starting to hum the mazurka from *Les Sylphides*, she began to dance.

But the sight of herself in a mirror made her laugh and she stopped and jumped into bed.

"Fancy doing *Sylphides* in pyjamas! I shall have to have practice clothes and shoes like Jenny, and later a tutu."

Life had never seemed so exciting before.

It was still exciting on Monday afternoon, when she slipped away from the classroom at ten minutes to four. The day had seemed interminable, but she had known better than to do badly at her work. If she got a bad report it might make her grandmother change her mind about the ballet lessons and that would be dreadful. So she had done a passable map, learned French verbs, and written about William the Conqueror, with all the time, at the very back of her mind, the thought of the coming interview with Madame.

She put on her outdoor clothes with fingers that trembled slightly and was relieved to see her grandmother's neat, straight figure waiting at the gate. Mrs Chester had put on her smartest coat, a fact which Drina noted with pleasure. It showed that she recognised the importance of the occasion.

The bus was not very full and they sat together in silence, Drina too excited to talk and her grandmother apparently with her thoughts far away. Drina led the way towards the Selswick School, for she had confessed on that night when she first asked for ballet lessons that she had been there with Jenny.

A porter in the hall looked out of his little cubby-hole and, on learning that Mrs Chester had an appointment with Miss Selswick, directed them to go up the stairs and turn to the left. They easily found the door marked "Office" and in there, talking to a girl who was probably her secretary, was Madame herself.

"It's the girl who came with Jenny Pilgrim!" she said, when she had greeted Mrs Chester. "What's your name, my dear?"

And before her grandmother could answer Drina said shyly but firmly, "Andrina Adamo, Madame."

"We usually call her Drina Adams, though," said Mrs Chester, equally firmly, and Madame looked interested, but was too tactful to ask questions then. She had learned to recognise resistance in parents and guardians, though more often they were all too eager for their children to be turned into famous ballerinas overnight.

She led them into an empty studio and asked Drina to take off her coat. Then she asked her to walk up and down and studied her very carefully.

"She's rather thin, but she looks healthy, and she has good limbs and poise, I think –"

"I want it to be clearly understood," said Mrs Chester pleasantly, "that Drina is to have ballet lessons purely for pleasure. There is no question of her ever wanting to be a dancer. It simply is that she wants to learn and, after due consideration, we have agreed to allow it for a time."

Miss Selswick looked from her to Drina.

"Yes, I see. But of course she'll have to work in my class. All the students work very hard, and most of them enjoy it. A good many of them, of course, hope to make dancing their career in time. Drina can certainly start after half-term, and she'll need practice clothes and shoes." She went into details, while Drina stood shifting from foot to foot, wishing that she could start that very afternoon.

Her grandmother's words had made her anxious and that anxiety made her pluck up courage, when they were on their way downstairs again, to gasp that she thought she had lost her handkerchief and dash away back to the studio. Miss Selswick was just coming out and she smiled very kindly at Drina.

"Did you – what's the matter, my child?"

"I just wanted to say," said Drina, facing her and feeling very small, for Madame was tall for a one-time ballet dancer, "that my grandmother didn't *quite* understand. It isn't purely for pleasure; honestly it isn't! You mustn't think that. I *will* like it: every minute of it. I just want to tell you that I'll work terribly hard, and – and I mean some day to be a real dancer. I don't care if I'm only in the corps de ballet, so long as I can dance. Jenny says you say only one in several thousand can ever hope to be a ballerina. Well, I don't care. I'd *like* to dance quite perfectly, and be great and famous. But if that's impossible, then I'll just dance. But I *will* work."

"Yes, I think you will," said Miss Selswick. "One in several thousand – yes, I often say that, and it's true. Anyway, we shall see, Andrina Adamo. Is that really your name, by the way?"

"Yes. My father was Italian."

"That accounts for your dark hair and eyes, then. He wasn't a dancer, was he?"

"Oh, no. He was a businessman from Milan." And then Drina saw her handkerchief on the floor, for it had genuinely been lost, gave Madame an odd, unpractised little curtsy, and flew off down the stairs.

Her grandmother was waiting in the hall, looking rather disapproving.

"What was all that about a handkerchief, Drina?"

Drina displayed it.

"I really had dropped it, Granny, but I wanted to speak to Madame, too. You see, I do really mean to work. It isn't just for pleasure. I mean to be a dancer, if I possibly can be by working hard."

"Well, don't forget you've got school to deal with as well," said Mrs Chester, after a very long pause. "And now we'll go and have some tea in a café. I need a cup badly."

She cannot have been annoyed with Drina, because she was very kind during tea, and Drina sat eating cream cakes and feeling settled and happy. Madame understood and all was well. And in only a very short time she would start learning to dance.

# 6
# Christmas

At last came the day when Drina was to have her first ballet lesson, and it must be admitted that, for one afternoon at least, her school work suffered. She was white and tense with excitement by four o'clock, and if her grandmother could have seen her she would have been more than ever sure that Drina ought not to go to the Selswick School. But she was not there to see, and only the class teacher, rather puzzled, remarked on her appearance.

"Aren't you well, Drina?"

"Oh, yes, quite well, thank you, Miss Rigby," said Drina.

"She's just excited," said the understanding Jenny. "She's starting to learn ballet dancing this afternoon, Miss Rigby. With Madame at the Selswick School, you know."

Miss Rigby did know and usually regarded the few absorbed dancers in the school with some regret. Ballet belonged to a separate world, and its pursuit so often resulted, in the really keen, in making school life seem less important. But she had noticed since the beginning of term that Drina Adams moved with a rare grace and she had heard from Miss MacDonnell that the girl had taken to Scottish dancing very much like a duck to water. Here, perhaps, was a born dancer and it was probably small use regretting it, if regret were necessary. So she looked at the little pale face, the big dark eyes and swinging black hair and then smiled.

"Well, I hope you enjoy it. I believe it is very hard work."

"Horribly!" agreed Jenny, pulling a face. "But Drina won't mind. *She* won't think it a bore just to practise standing correctly at the *barre* for hours and hours, or practising one little leg movement over and over again. I always stand wrongly, Miss Rigby, in spite of all Madame says. Either I hollow my back and my tail sticks out, or I stick my stomach out and everything else gets in a wrong position. I'm hopeless, but Drina won't be."

"She always stands very well, it seems to me," said Miss Rigby and dismissed them.

Jenny and Drina put on their things hastily and flew towards the bus stop. Jenny was actually in no hurry, but Drina was determined to be at the Selswick School with plenty of time to spare. Not that she could do anything at the *barre* until Madame came, she supposed, but she must be there.

She changed into her practice clothes in eager haste and tied back her hair with a piece of red ribbon. She waited impatiently for Jenny, who was chattering with some older girls.

There seemed to be one or two other new ones and Drina looked at them curiously. One was a pretty girl of about her own age, who was slouching up against the cloakroom wall.

"The doctor said I'm to learn ballet," she explained, in answer to someone's question. "He says it will help my tendency to knock-knees. I do hope Madame isn't too cross and stern."

The other was a rather gawky girl a year or two older, who was announcing that she had had a few lessons in Manchester. They had just moved south, it seemed, and she had promptly been enrolled at the Selswick School.

They all went upstairs together, Drina quite silent, for she was savouring the deep pleasure of being part

of the Dancing School. No longer an outsider, in a thick coat and clumsy outdoor shoes, but a prospective dancer, scantily clad and light in ballet shoes.

She never forgot the satisfaction of that first hour, though it consisted of little more than standing at the *barre* and in learning some of the ballet terms, all of them French, as she had realised on her first visit to Madame's class. Several of the more skilful beginners had moved out of the class at half-term, but Jenny, of course, was still there, and still, as she had said in school, standing badly.

"No one can ever get far," said Madame, standing over her and indicating again and again the right position, "until correct placing is learned. Jenny, you're *still* sticking out your tail, my child!"

Drina was conscious of nothing but Madame's words and her own beautiful movements, of the *barre* under her hands and the happy knowledge that she had started at last.

At the end of the class Madame put her hands on her shoulders.

"That is the beginning, Drina, my child. You stand well already, but you must practise continually. Even the highly skilled dancer, the greatest of ballerinas, does the basic exercises at the *barre* every day of her dancing life."

"Yes, Madame. I will remember," Drina said eagerly, and she went home to have her tea and do her homework in a haze of pleasure and resolution.

Mrs Pilgrim, in her anxiety that Jenny should succeed, had provided a practice room at home. It was a bare little room, with little in it but a *barre* and record player. Jenny regarded it as a necessary evil, like homework, but Drina was grateful and enchanted to be able to use it. She took to going home with Jenny every afternoon when there was not a ballet class and together they did their exercises and sometimes listened to records of ballet music. Jenny was bored with the music and often left her alone, but Drina never tired of the lovely music of *Les Sylphides, Giselle* and many other ballets that she had not seen and could scarcely imagine.

So the weeks passed and end of term and Christmas loomed ahead. At school, Drina was very busy and she still enjoyed most of the lessons. She was developing a personality and was popular with most of the girls, though there were one or two who resented her occasional remoteness and dreaminess and who thought her stuck up. Jenny continued to be her greatest friend and they understood each other very thoroughly, which was satisfactory for both of them.

Jenny was genuinely pleased that Drina had got her wish and was learning to dance, and she was too open-hearted and intelligent to mind the fact that her friend was already making progress while she herself was still finding the most elementary exercises difficult.

"Madame knows I don't want to learn," she said gloomily one day, when they were walking home from school with their heads bent against a bitter December wind. "I wish she'd tell Mother definitely that it's no good."

Drina was looking forward to Christmas. There was to be a party at School, and she had received invitations to private parties as well. Jenny was to have one two days after Christmas, and there would be at least half a dozen others during the holidays. When Mrs Chester saw all the invitations, she said that Drina must give a party, too, and the date was fixed for January 3rd.

But the thing that Drina found most exciting was the

thought of the Christmas Show at the Selswick School. This would take place on December 23rd and the main part of the display was to be a ballet composed by Madame and one of her assistants, Monsieur Fiendé, *Snow White and the Seven Dwarfs*. This gave a large number of the ballet pupils a part, though some roles were very small. The role of Snow White went to a beautiful girl of twelve, Shirley Merrin, who was already a very good dancer, and the Queen was, of course, one of the star pupils, a dark, handsome girl of fifteen. Jenny had a small part as a rabbit, but Drina had no part at all, as she had joined the school so late and was very much a beginner. That, however, did not really worry her, as there would be other shows. By the time the much bigger Summer Show came round she would surely have a chance to dance a little in public? As it was, it was enough to be part of the school and to know that she could help with selling programmes and showing people to their seats.

She was rather afraid that her grandmother would refuse to go to the show, as she had preserved a slightly disapproving attitude whenever Drina mentioned dancing, but she took a ticket and seemed to intend to go.

"Next year *I* shall be dancing!" said Drina, making an attempt at a *pirouette*.

But in the end she got a small part in *Snow White*, for one of the Queen's attendants went down with flu at the last minute. Her dress, which had fortunately been at the Selswick School, just fitted Drina and she looked charming in it. She only had to dance a very few steps, but it was fun to be in the ballet, and deeply satisfying, too.

The dress was a crisp white one, rather long and full, and her hair was bound with silver ribbon.

"So much more romantic-looking than being an idiotic rabbit!" said Jenny admiringly on the night, when they were all in the dressing-rooms.

"I thought you liked country things?" said Drina, giggling.

"Well, I do. And it really suits me better than anything else, except perhaps being a dwarf." But Jenny, for all her practical common sense, stifled a faint sigh that she was plump and ungraceful and one of the worst pupils in the school.

The ballet was a great success. Most of the students looked charming, the music was attractive, and there were many skilful dancers in the Selswick School, even though Madame knew that so few of them could ever hope to reach the status of ballerina.

Drina enjoyed herself thoroughly and was, in fact, so happy that she scarcely knew herself. It was her first taste of being made up and appearing on a stage, even though it was only the stage in the little theatre on the ground floor of the Selswick School.

Mrs Chester, sitting a trifle grimly in the third row, made little comment about the dancing, but she told Drina that she looked very nice.

"Only I hope you won't spend too much time practising in the holidays. What you need is a good rest and some fun, Drina dear," she said on the way home.

"But dancing *is* fun!" said Drina, still partly lost in a world of palaces and woodland and music that had grown beloved and familiar, for she had watched the ballet often, though only getting her part at the very last moment.

The next day Jenny came round to Beech Road, looking startled and rather triumphant.

"Drina! Drina! You'll never guess!"

"What?" Drina demanded, as she took her up to her

room to see her Christmas cards and early presents.

"Madame spoke to Mother last night and I think she's really convinced at last that I'm not cut out for dancing. I don't believe I shall go back to the Selswick School."

Drina stared at her in deep dismay.

"Oh, but you must! I'd miss you dreadfully, and –"

Jenny plumped herself down on the bed.

"You wouldn't miss me for long. You're at home there now and you're going to be all right. And of course we'll see plenty of each other otherwise, and you can still come and practise at my house. Oh, I shall be so glad not to have to think of placing my body correctly, and all those awful positions of the arms and legs! I can just be sturdy and unimaginative and myself!"

Drina, at the back of her mind, continued to be rather dismayed, but the news did not really spoil her Christmas. After all, it was true she was at home at the Selswick School and she certainly did not really need Jenny's company, though it had been fun to have it.

She was quite friendly with another ten-year-old called Joy Kelly, and with a boy of nine-and-a-half called Mark Playford, whom everyone thought would soon be a promising dancer. There were others that she did not care for, including the fair girl she had thought smug on her first visit to the school. She was an assured person and keen on her work, though inclined to resent criticism. Her name was Daphne Daniety and she was one of the students who were sure that they would go a long way. If Madame was not so convinced she did not say much, for Daphne was only a beginner and had years of hard and intensive work before her before there could be any conclusive result.

Daphne always seemed rather jealous of Drina and

sometimes went out of her way to say cutting things. But Drina, while being sensitive, was not usually very upset, because Daphne was not popular in any case and was rather a lonely member of the class.

Christmas really was a lovely time. The weather was sunny and rather warm at first, but by New Year's Eve it had turned frosty and crisp, and a full moon hung over the town as Drina and her grandparents came home from the pantomime.

It had been exciting to be in the Grand Theatre again, but, remembering the magic of that first night of real ballet, Drina found the pantomime rather disappointing. There had been too many funny men and not enough emphasis on the fairy story. But the dancing interested her, and it was fun as well as instructive to watch the girls that she knew by sight. For several members of the Selswick School had been given short engagements, and she envied them their experience of the small, draughty dressing-rooms and the thrill of hearing the words, "Beginners, please!"

They took Jenny with them, and Jenny thoroughly enjoyed the funny men and hardly seemed to regret the lack of story. She was knowledgeable and scornful about the dancing, which certainly was of a low standard on the whole.

Mrs Chester looked at her slightly disapprovingly and would perhaps have liked to point out that little girls of ten should not be so ready to air their opinions in the hearing of the people in front and on either side.

After that the holidays flew by, with parties and sliding on the pond in the park, and a trip to Jenny's uncle's farm in the Pilgrims' car. Drina enjoyed seeing the farm, and the beauty of the wintry woods and fields made her catch her breath more than once. She liked seeing the cows and pigs, too, and she enjoyed scrambling up to the top of the stacked hay by way of a shaky ladder, but, unlike Jenny, she did not feel any real kinship with the smell of animals and straw, with mud and cold and clanging buckets.

Her mind began to turn again towards the coming term at Elleray and the Selswick School, and she practised diligently every day at the *barre* in Jenny's house. Afterwards, the two would sprawl on the rug, chattering about all sorts of things.

The snow was deep on the morning that they went back to school, but it was clearing a little by the time Drina was due to go for her first lesson with Madame; to her great relief, for she had been afraid that her grandmother would say she ought not to go in bad weather.

She returned to the Selswick School without Jenny, but with eagerness and a light heart. It was wonderful to enter the hall again, to grin at old Hobbs, the porter, and to fly down the stairs into the dark and rather stuffy cloakrooms, where the others were all talking about what they had done during the holidays.

And to be back at the *barre* in the big, light studio was like returning home. Drina savoured it all and got down to work with a will, gradually mastering the basic movements and positions and feeling that she could use her body with greater ease as the weeks passed.

# 7

# "The Changeling"

Life was very full for Drina; too full, her grandmother often said. But, apart from a cold during February, which kept her at home for an interminable week, she was very well and was even putting on a little weight. Her arms and legs were no longer quite so thin and she carried her head very well on her slim white neck.

She knew that Madame approved of her, though she did not always spare her criticism. But any hard words she might speak were usually deserved and their only result was to make Drina work harder than ever. Joy Kelly and Daphne Daniety were working hard, too, and before many months had passed Daphne and Drina were inclined to be rivals. Not that the feeling originated with Drina, but she was conscious of it and the fact that Daphne was pleased if she ever fell below Madame's high and exacting standard.

Easter passed and the gardens on the outskirts of the town were colourful and sweet-smelling with wallflowers. The trees were greener every day and some of the girls at Elleray School were already appearing in the green dresses that were part of the summer uniform.

At the Selswick School excitement began to run high as plans for the Summer Show were made. The main part of the display was to be a ballet called *The Changeling*, again composed by Madame and M Feindé. This was to be for the younger students, and those over twelve or thirteen were to do one called *Midsummer Madness*.

The younger pupils were gathered together and told the story of *The Changeling* and Drina's imagination was immediately fired. She knew that she would have a part, but had no idea which it might be amongst so many. *The Changeling* was about a large family of children, all fair and merry, who lived in a cottage at the edge of a wood. They were fond of playing in the heart of the wood, in spite of the fact that their mother had warned them again and again of the gnomes and fairies that lived there and might perhaps harm them or play tricks on them. The fairest and merriest child was the least afraid and she loved to slip out of her bed and dance alone in the moonlight. One night when she was dancing she found herself surrounded by a fairy company and could not escape. They took her away, but left in her place a changeling, a strange, dark-haired, dark-eyed child, as different as could be from the real child, Selina.

The changeling was wild and mischievous and her new family could not understand her at all. They wanted Selina back and tried again and again to reach her in her fairy haunts. But, though Selina danced in the wood with her fairy captors every night, she could not escape, until one night a little prince, from the nearby palace, saw her and helped her to run away.

They reached the cottage together, and the changeling, after one look at Selina, danced away to join her own people, while Selina, her sisters and her mother joined in a final joyous dance with the little prince.

Immediately, Drina could see the whole ballet and especially the odd little changeling, with her mischievous smile and flying black hair. But it was a tremendous shock, when the lists were read out, to find her name called.

"Me?" she cried incredulously. "Me the changeling? Oh, Madame!"

And Madame, smiling at her very kindly, said, "We think you can do it, Drina, and you will certainly look the part. You are to wear bright red and have your hair loose. But of course, as you know, you will have to work very hard."

Daphne had been scowling, but she was thoroughly mollified to find herself with the role of Selina. Joy was to be one of the sisters and was quite thrilled about that, while Mark Playford was to dance the little prince.

"All the same I don't see why *you* should have the name part!" Daphne said, as they all streamed away to the cloakrooms. "You only came last October."

"Well, *you* couldn't have had it," Joy pointed out. "Not unless you dyed your hair. And after all, you've got a really good part. Besides, Drina dances marvellously already. I don't know how she does it."

The dances for the ballet were quite simple and Drina found that there was nothing she would not be able to manage so long as she practised continually throughout the weeks of the summer term.

She was in the seventh heaven to find herself the changeling and the only thing that occasionally made her unhappy was her grandmother's reserve on the subject. Her grandfather, on hearing the news, gave her some chocolates and congratulated her very heartily, but her grandmother merely said:

"Well, don't let your school work suffer, please, Drina." And she added to Drina's sharp dismay,

"Sometimes I think this dancing business has gone quite far enough. You think of nothing else. It can't be good for you."

"But I *have* to think about it," Drina said, standing on one foot. "I mean to be a dancer, Granny." And then she wished that she had not said it, for, as usual, her grandmother's face took on the closed-up look and she left the sitting-room abruptly.

Perhaps to counteract the hours spent working and dancing, Mrs Chester took Drina out more than usual that summer, and at half-term they went down to the South Coast for a long weekend. It was lovely to be by the sea and to go running along the shore, leaping the salty pools, but Drina was glad to be home again and continuing the rehearsals for *The Changeling*, which was taking shape very rapidly.

She loved the music, especially the music for her first dance in the wood, when she was left there in place of Selina, and sometimes it really seemed to her that she was the fairy child, dark and alien. Once she overheard Madame saying something about her having a strong dramatic sense as well as the makings of a really good dancer and her heart lifted. But, of course, there were days when things did not go so well, and then Daphne looked triumphant and Drina was sad, though always determined to do better at future rehearsals.

She had an understudy, another dark girl called Cherry, but there seemed no danger that Cherry would get the part, a fact that she did not seem to mind particularly. For Cherry was playing a fairy in any case and was not particularly ambitious.

The red dress, designed by Madame, was being made by a dressmaker in the town, for Mrs Chester was not very fond of sewing, though she liked embroidery and knitting. Daphne's dress was to be blue, while those of her sisters were to be in corresponding shades of yellow, green, pink and mauve. It was only the changeling, so dark and so different, who was to wear a really hard, bright colour.

All this time Jenny had been kept in touch with the Selswick School through Drina's endless chatter and her own occasional visits as a spectator at the ballet classes. She did not seem to regret her abandoned lessons at all, and she thoroughly enjoyed hearing about the progress of *The Changeling* and the jealousies and small triumphs that went on at the Dancing School.

"I'd sooner you than me," she said one day, as she and Drina lay out on the lawn. It was already July and the weather had turned hot and bright. "But I'm certainly coming to watch, so get me a ticket. Actually, Mother wants one, too. She seems to be resigned to not having a ballet-dancing daughter, and she said the other day that she wants to see you dance. After all, it's your first big part, and you're sure to have quite a triumph."

"Madame says we're not to set too much store by any praise we may get," Drina said prudently. "She says parents always make a fuss and think we're perfect, but really we're very far from being that."

"How like Madame!" Jenny said, chewing grass. "Anyway, whatever she says, I shall clap you for as long as possible and send you some flowers."

The days were too full for them to pass slowly, but all the same there were times when Drina thought that July 22nd would never come.

The dress rehearsal went off not too badly and Madame gáve Drina and Daphne comforting words of praise. Drina was pleased and excited, but all the same she was horribly conscious as she made her way home that she did not feel very well. Perhaps it was just that she was too worked up about the show and she was afraid to say anything to her grandmother. But by the time she went to bed, she felt really ill and her neck hurt alarmingly. It was quite swollen, too, and, though she hoped fervently that she would feel better in the morning, she awoke several times in the night feeling worse and worse.

It was quite an effort to get up the next morning and when she looked in the mirror, she gave a gasp of horror, for her face and neck were dreadfully swollen. She looked simply hideous as well as feeling extremely ill.

But she washed and dressed and went down to breakfast, trying frantically to assure herself that she would be all right soon. However, her grandmother gave her one glance and cried out in dismay.

"Drina! My dear child! Why didn't you call me? You must go back to bed at once and I'll telephone the doctor. You must have mumps, I'm afraid. I'd heard that there were several cases in the town."

Drina held the back of her chair and said in a wobbly voice, "Granny, I can't! I can't have mumps! Think of *The Changeling*! It's tonight!"

"I can't help that, though I admit it's hard," said her grandmother, her voice softening. "Off you go, Drina, and I'll get Mrs Tring to fill you a hot water bottle. It's chilly this morning and you're shivering. You've probably got a temperature. Oh, dear me! When we'd arranged to go to Wales next week, too!"

Drina crept back upstairs and was very thankful, in spite of her dismay, to lie down again. When the doctor came he was very nice and most sympathetic, but he confirmed that she had mumps and must stay in bed for some time.

"I'm sorry about that dancing display, but it's the sort of thing that happens in this life, more's the pity. You'll just have to grin and bear it, though I'm afraid that grinning will hurt you rather a lot for the next few days!"

So Drina, inconsolable, lay there all day, feeling more and more ill and in pain. Occasionally, the telephone bell shrilled below, and on one occasion her grandmother came up to bring her a note from Jenny and a lovely bunch of red roses.

"Jenny seems really upset. I must say she's a nice child. She says she's had mumps and wants to see you, but I said you were much too poorly to have visitors for a few days."

"But Madame – what did Madame say?" Drina croaked.

"She said she was extremely sorry, and she hopes you'll soon be feeling better. A child called Cherry is going to dance your part and they're having an extra rehearsal this afternoon if they can get all the dancers together."

So that night Drina, feverish and unhappy, pictured over and over again the scene at the Selswick School and Cherry wearing the red dress, which had been left at the school after the dress rehearsal. It was her first big disappointment and one she was never to forget.

But the next morning came a comforting note from Madame and some beautiful flowers. The Show had been quite a success and Cherry had acquitted herself well on the whole.

After a few days, Drina was able to feel philosophical, but it was a depressing time and she was glad when Jenny could come and cheer her up. No one could stay sad for long when Jenny was there.

# 8

# Drina's Triumph

The holiday in North Wales had to be postponed for quite a while and by the time that Drina was able to go about again, free from infection, nearly all her friends had gone away. Even Jenny was away by then, at her uncle's farm, but it had been arranged that Drina should join her there after the fortnight in Wales.

At last came the day when Drina and her grandparents travelled North. They went by car, but even so it was a long awkward journey, and it was getting towards sunset as they headed across the Lleyn Peninsula towards the tiny village of Porth-din-Lleyn. The Snowdon peaks were behind them and they were in a country of earthen "hedges" and small, whitewashed farms, with, for a long time, no sign of the sea.

Drina was tired by then, for she did not much care for car journeys and she was still not very well. It was partly that she was still upset by the whole business of getting mumps at such an unfortunate time, and she had never really recovered her spirits. But suddenly, after asking the way, they took a narrow, winding, bumpy track over what seemed to be a golf course on a curving headland and the sea was very near. There was a little rocky bay immediately below, with the sea breaking in white foam on a tiny beach.

Then suddenly, they were dropping sharply through a sort of cutting in the cliff, and Drina had just time to cry, "There can't be a village anywhere here!" when they were actually on the shore and she saw Porth-din-Lleyn.

"I believe that one can actually approach from the Nevin side at low tide by driving over the sand," said her grandfather.

Drina was suddenly enchanted. It was almost an unreal scene, like a set for a ballet. The tiny, remote village on the shore, with the cottage doors actually opening on to the beach; the little harbour, topped by the high cliffs of the continuing headland; the mountains away across the green water, faintly rose-tinted by the reflection of the sunset.

It was a dream place, far from the world; certainly far from flat, green Warwickshire. And before she crept into bed in her little room that looked towards the bobbing boats in the harbour, Drina knew that she would love it.

The next morning, she was up early and out before her grandparents had stirred. Smoke rose from the little stone houses and an emerald boat was heading away round the headland. The nearest mountain – Yr Eifel, her grandfather had told her it was called – dropped sheer to the sea round the curve of the bay, and the whole scene glittered and sparkled, vividly colourful in the morning light.

Drina found the cutting down which they had driven the previous night and was soon high on the headland, standing on the cliff-edge immediately above some of the small, crouching cottages. The warm sea breeze lifted her pink cotton dress and took her heavy hair back from her face.

It was perfect! It was heaven! And behind her stretched the grass of the headland, in places as smooth as a dancing floor. Drina kicked off her sandals and began to dance there, lifting her face to the sun and raising her arms with that grace that was partly natural and partly the result of months of exercises.

She felt happy and released and, dancing there, with the dark blue sea on three sides, she wondered how she had ever been miserable. There would be other shows at the Selswick School and, after all, she was still not quite eleven. There would be years and years of shows, in fact, and they might even do *The Changeling* again one day.

The thing to do now was to have a holiday and grow brown and strong, ready for the new term when it came.

Mrs Chester was much relieved at the change in her and each day, while her husband played golf with some acquaintances that he had made, she suggested new excursions for herself and Drina. They went into Nevin, and once to the lovely little village of Aberdaron, where they watched the boat from Bardsey Island come in; they walked along the shore and bathed in the surprisingly warm sea.

But several times, Mr Chester left his golf and took them out in the car. Once, they drove as far as they could up a steep lane and then Drina and her grandfather climbed Yr Eifel to the very top, revelling in the vast view of the Lleyn Peninsula below. Another day, they went to Beddgelert and on to Caernarvon, where Drina was thrilled to see the huge, romantic castle, with its gates and walls and towers.

There were times when Drina longed for Jenny's lively company, but on the whole she enjoyed herself and it was good to be alone sometimes, free to scramble on the rocks and sit with her bare brown feet in warm pools. Sometimes, when she knew herself quite alone, she broke into dance movements, but she did not speak much of dancing. It was something that was always there at the back of her mind, something that she would go back to with joy and relief, but, meanwhile, she was on holiday and Wales, in the continuing sunlight, was a lovely country.

She was sorry when the time came to leave the village on the shore and she vowed to herself that one day she would come back to see what it was like when the wild seas of winter broke close to the little houses. But it was fun to know that she was going to join Jenny, and when, at last, the car drew up at the farm and Jenny came running across the yard, tousled, suntanned and as lively as ever, Drina felt very happy.

Mr and Mrs Chester were invited in for a cup of tea, but they did not stay long, and then Jenny was free to take Drina all over the farm and the surrounding fields. Finally, they flung themselves down at the edge of the corn stubble and gave themselves up to gossip. Drina told all about Wales and how she had sometimes danced on the headland, and Jenny about her trips to Stratford, Warwick and the Cotswolds.

"Grandfather promised me that I should go to the Memorial Theatre this summer, but I haven't been yet," Drina said.

Jenny answered easily, "Oh, well, you'd probably be bored. Shakespeare's awfully heavy mostly, isn't he? Or p'rhaps we're not old enough. Besides, they aren't doing *The Dream*. That's what you wanted to see, isn't it? I expect he'll take you another year."

Drina began to find herself really fascinated with the life of the farm, but she knew that she would never be so caught up in it as Jenny was. Jenny felt about the

farm as Drina felt about dancing and was never too tired to fetch the cows, collect eggs or feed and water the hens.

They were very happy and busy, but they lazed occasionally, too, sometimes on top of bales of hay and more often in the fields from which most of the corn had now been harvested.

One day, Drina leaped up and began to dance, humming to herself, and Jenny lay and watched her for some time.

"Wow! How you have improved! Do you know, Drina, I believe you're a born dancer."

Drina stopped abruptly, flushed and suddenly shy.

"Oh, Jenny, do you really think so? It sounds so lovely!"

Jenny sat amongst the last of the poppies and stared up at her. Her plump, rosy face was graver than usual.

"It's a sort of feeling I've got. Almost like a – a premonition. I believe you'll be great and famous. I believe that one day I shall be proud to say, 'Andrina Adamo, the great ballerina? Oh, yes, I used to know her well. We went to school together.'"

"Oh, Jenny, don't be silly! I've got to work for five more years at least, and *then*, at the very best, I shall only be in a *corps de ballet*."

"At first of course you will. But you'll go on. Gipsy Jenny tells you so. Cross me 'and wiv silver, lady!"

Drina laughed, but she was for a moment carried away into a dream of success. Her name in lights; in the ballet books, like those great ones, Markova, Dolin, Fonteyn, Ivory. She had read a good deal about them now and what they had done for their art. Might people one day say that Adamo, like Ivory, had made dancing a perfect thing?

Then she shook herself and laughed again, remembering how little she knew and how hard she would have to work to get anywhere at all, and they went home to eat a huge tea in the farmhouse kitchen and then to help to feed the young pigs.

Once back at school and Madame's classes, the holidays seemed infinitely far away to Drina, though she sometimes thought of the beauty of Porth-din-Lleyn; the little coves, the smooth, bright sea, and the blue, distant mountains.

At school, she was moved up into 2A and was with Jenny again, for Jenny, some months older, but not so clever, had gone into the higher class the previous April. The temporary parting in school had made no real difference to their freindship, but it was good to be sitting side by side again.

At the Selswick School, Drina immediately found herself deep in hard work, which was how she wanted things to be. She was definitely making progress and was a better dancer than most of the others of her own age. Not that Madame always spared her her most stringent criticisms; in fact, she was sometimes harder on Drina than on the others, but she very occasionally praised her, too, and that was the thing that lifted Drina to heights of greatest happiness.

It was a bad autumn, bitterly cold and with rain day after day, but Drina was very well and would arrive home after the ballet classes with glowing cheeks, plodding up the path in her raincoat, hood and boots. She was rarely tired and certainly never when it was a question of dancing.

About the middle of October, when Madame was starting to make definite plans for the Christmas Show, one student after another went down with flu and some schools in the town eventually closed. There were several cases at Elleray School, but it stayed open and Drina was glad. A holiday would mean that she could practise more, but even so life was better when it was completed by school. She could enjoy her own company, but as she grew older she was beginning to find the house in Beech Road rather dull and lonely. Her grandmother was very much absorbed in her various clubs and societies, and her grandfather was in London more and more often, on business for the firm. She wished, not for the first time, that she had a crowd of brothers like Jenny. She had long since ceased to be shy with the Pilgrim boys, and they in their turn, accepted her as "not a bad kid", but it was not like having a brother, or, better still, a sister, who would be on hand to talk to at bedtime and in the mornings.

The flu epidemic grew to such proportions that Madame decided that there was no point in trying to organise the Christmas Show. Drina was disappointed, of course, but what really mattered was that nothing had happened to stop the actual classes, though their numbers were greatly depleted.

Christmas approached and then passed. For a few weeks, the Warwickshire countryside was white with the heaviest snow for years and then, suddenly, there was a feeling of spring. The daffodil shoots were pushing up in gardens and the wind had a softer touch.

"Spring!" thought Drina, sniffing the air, and doing a few dancing steps along the quiet pavement.

"Spring!" thought Jenny, and she pictured the farm: the young lambs skipping in the fields and the bright blades of the winter wheat growing ever higher and more sturdy. Jenny had a very strong feeling for the changing seasons, far stronger than Drina, who now thought of the passing year mainly in terms of the Selswick School.

In April, another ballet company came to Willerbury and Jenny and Drina went alone on Saturday afternoon. They saw *La Boutique Fantasque*, *Façade* and one act of *Swan Lake* and once more Drina was transported into what she felt, strangely, was the real world. Jenny was rather bored, but was too good a theatregoer to wriggle, and, in gratitude for her company, Drina went with her to see a Western the following week.

When early summer came, Madame told her pupils that they were going to revive *Snow White* for the Summer Show, and there was much speculation as to who would get the main parts. The girl who had originally danced the Queen was now in the *corps de ballet* of a well known company and Shirley Merrin's family had moved to London. She had recently won a scholarship to the Royal Ballet School, a piece of news that had filled many hearts with envy, though everyone knew that she deserved her good fortune.

Daphne was convinced that she would be chosen to

dance Snow White.

"But she won't," Joy Kelly said emphatically. "She's getting tall for her age, and she isn't improving as much as she should."

"How awful to grow tall!" cried Drina, for it was the dread of many of the girls, particularly the older ones, that they would exceed the height suitable for a ballet dancer.

"Don't worry. You won't. Why, you're still positively tiny for nearly twelve. That's one of the things you don't have to bother about."

When the names were announced Drina was Snow White and she was both enchanted and appalled. It was a big part, far bigger than her role as the changeling, and she could not forgot that she had let the school down once. But when she said so tentatively to Madame, she laughed.

"My dear Drina, you can do it if you work, and I can't believe that fate could be so unkind as to strike you down with chickenpox or measles."

"But there are still plenty –" Drina began.

"Shhh, my child! You are in good health and there's no reason at all why you should be unlucky twice. I want you to dance Snow White and Daphne will understudy you."

Daphne, of course, was sulky and difficult, but not in front of Madame. She was far too much in awe of her for that.

"Serves you right!" said the outspoken Joy. "You're too conceited for words, and you've been horrid to Drina. We're all really pleased, Drina! It's a lovely part."

It *was* a lovely role and Drina was wildly happy, so happy and so caught up in the ballet that it must be admitted her school work suffered, and on one occasion she was summoned to the headmistress's room to give an explanation.

After that, she did try to work harder and with more concentration, but the only really important thing seemed to be the growing shape of *Snow White*.

As June and July passed, she was more and more at the Selswick School in the afternoons after school and on Saturdays, and Mrs Chester was frankly disapproving.

"Drina, you will simply have to come out with me after school and get some new summer clothes and sandals. I've suggested it several times and you've got out of it. You really can't go on like this."

"Only till *Snow White* is over, Granny!" said Drina. "It's getting better and better and I do love it so."

"I don't know why Madame gave you that big part. She knows quite well that you aren't dancing seriously and it would have been better to give it to a child who means to make ballet her career."

Drina gulped and tried to speak, but then remained silent. What was the good of arguing? So she went down town meekly enough with her grandmother and three new dresses were bought for her, as well as a pair of sandals for summer wear.

Drina was so absorbed during the last few weeks of the summer term that she did not even notice the change of atmosphere in her home. There was far more post than usual, various strangers came to the house, and her grandfather looked worried and sometimes glanced at her with more than a troubled expression. There was no mention of holidays, either, though usually they made plans quite early on.

But Drina was blissfully unaware of it all. She came running home one evening, a week or so before the Show, with a handful of tickets.

"Granny! Grandfather! You'll both come, won't you? I've reserved seats for you in the second row. You've never seen me dance. Being the Queen's attendant that time didn't count. I'd only just started then."

"Yes, we'll come," said her grandfather, before his wife could speak. "Of course, Drina."

"And Mrs Pilgrim and Jenny are coming, too."

Drina felt that she ought to keep her fingers crossed, but nothing happened to prevent her dancing that time. The evening of the Summer Show came and she was in one of the crowded dressing-rooms, putting on her brief white dress and being made up by one of the assistants. She felt nervous, of course, but it was an exciting sort of feeling.

Then the music of the ballet began and the curtain rose. And after that Drina thought of nothing but being Snow White. She was only dimly conscious of the packed audience.

She put her whole heart into her dancing and was so light and graceful, so appealing in her smallness, with her black hair flying out in a short cloud, that she was a success almost from the start, though she did not realise it until the curtain went down at the end and the applause broke out. Some people were actually calling her name and one of the voices sounded like Jenny's, but there were others, too. "Andrina Adamo" had been put in the programme, and it had been a great thrill to see her full name there, in print for the first time.

"Andrina!"

There were many curtains and Drina and the Queen took some of them alone. Then Drina was pushed forward and she stood there curtsying and blushing, so very happy that it seemed as though it must all be a dream.

She was still in a sort of delicious haze when her grandfather drove them home, and she scarcely noticed her grandmother's silence nor the slight atmosphere of tension.

She drank her milk and ate some biscuits still without noticing and presently asked, "Oh, Granny! Grandfather! Did you like it? I know it wasn't much really. Not like a real theatre and a real audience. But – oh, one day perhaps I *shall* dance in a real theatre! Only it will be years and years yet, unless I get an engagement like some of the others. I can try next year, of course. But I shall have to keep on working under Madame until –"

"No, Drina, I'm afraid you won't," said her grandmother very quietly, and in a voice that shook very slightly.

Drina opened her eyes wide and for the first time began to feel frightened.

"What do you mean, Granny? I'll never go to anyone but Madame. She knows – she doesn't like us to change, except to go to one of the big schools, like the Royal Ballet School or the Dominick."

"Perhaps not until tomorrow," said Mr Chester, very quietly. "The child's over-excited, and –"

"I didn't mean to tell her till tomorrow, but she may as well know, as she brought the subject up. Drina, perhaps we should have told you sooner, but we were waiting till everything was settled. We're leaving Willerbury and going back to London. This house is sold and we've a big flat in Westminster, near the river."

Drina went absolutely white and sat down very suddenly on the sofa.

"I don't – believe it! You couldn't! It can't be true!"

# 9
# Goodbye to the Selswick School

"It can't be true!" Drina said again, when she had got her breath. She felt sick and her hands were clammy.

"I'm afraid it *is* true," her grandfather said gently. "But you'll have to be brave, Drina, and make the best of things. Think of the fun of living in London and –"

"Brave! There's no question of her having to be brave," said Mrs Chester very briskly, though her eyes were anxious. "She'll miss her friends at first, of course, but Jenny can come and stay whenever she likes in the holidays, and Drina'll soon make new friends. We're arranging for you to go to a very good school, Drina. You'll enjoy living in London and learning to find your way about. Think –"

"But –" Drina was still stunned, still sick. "I can't go to London! I must stay with Madame. My – my whole career depends on her, and –"

"Now listen, Drina," her grandmother said, quite kindly but still briskly. "You knew when you started dancing that is was only for pleasure. I told Madame myself. There's never been the slightest thought of your taking it up as a career. Just lately especially you've given the whole business far too much time and thought. Your school work has obviously suffered;

your report was not nearly as good as usual. You've had your wish and have learned to dance and that must be the end of it. We don't mean to be hard or unkind, but you're a sensible girl at heart and —"

"But I must be a dancer! I *can* if I work. Didn't you think I danced quite well tonight? Weren't you pleased?"

She did not understand the nameless expression that flitted over her grandmother's face, nor the strange note in her voice.

"Yes, you danced very nicely indeed, but we don't want this little show to go to your head, do we? You danced quite well, and you're very graceful and much better in health than you were. Now you must learn to enjoy other things." Then suddenly her voice grew much warmer. "Oh, Drina, we'd never hear of you having a ballet dancer's life. We care far too much for you for that. It's drudgery and gives so little time for ordinary living. And there are so many other things in life —"

"I only care about dancing," said Drina. "Oh, Granny, if we must go to London perhaps I could have an audition for the Royal Ballet School or the Dominick one. Madame would recommend me, I'm sure. Oh, Granny! Grandfather —"

"Calm yourself, Drina. We have no intention of asking Madame for any such recommendation. You have your school work to do, and you'll really enjoy exploring London."

"But why? But why? Why are we going? I don't understand!"

"Your grandfather had the offer of an excellent post at the London office. Far better than he has here, for it's only a small branch office. And we thought that the change would do us all good. After all, we are

Londoners and, as luck would have it, we heard of the ideal flat. There's a lovely little room that will just do for you, looking over the river and with just a glimpse of the Houses of Parliament. You'll love it, Drina."

But Drina's alarm and despair were so deep that she could not take in the words.

"I won't go! I'll go and live with Jenny! It's cruel and wrong and I won't leave Madame! She won't let me, anyway."

"Madame will get a letter in the morning explaining the position. She'll understand that people must move —"

"I *won't* go! Or if I must I'll have to have an audition. I shall die if I don't!" And she was away up the stairs into her own room, where she locked the door and flung herself down on her bed.

Her grandfather knocked quietly ten minutes later, and, after a few moments, Drina let him in.

He sat down on the edge of the bed and spoke gravely:

"It is hard, Drina, but life is full of difficult situations, I'm afraid. We certainly are going to London in three or four weeks' time, and —"

"I could bear that," Drina said, sniffing. "But not doing without dancing. Oh, Grandfather —"

"Now listen, my poppet. I know you think we are cruel and unfeeling just now, but if you think about it carefully when you're calmer you'll see that your grandmother is right. She cares for you very deeply — after all, she's brought you up since you were only eighteen months old — and she wants you to have the right kind of life. Neglecting your school work and having no time for ordinary fun isn't right, and we neither of us want you worrying about your career when you're not even twelve. We want you to have a

happy, easy time, and in London you can do a lot of exciting things. Then there'll be the new school and new friends. Do try and make the best of it, for your grandmother has made up her mind and she won't change it."

Drina looked into his kind, anxious face.

"*You* don't want me to stop dancing?"

"Well, not perhaps so violently as your grandmother wishes, but – yes, I do, Drina. I don't want you to give your life to being a dancer, and I *do* want you to do well at school –"

"I can do both! I'm clever. Everyone says so!"

"But you *have* neglected your work this term and you've done scarcely anything but think about *Snow White*. Honestly. Drina, it will be best in the long run. You'll see some day that we're right."

"I don't think I shall ever see it," Drina said drearily. "If I have to, I'll try, but –"

"Go to bed now. It's very late and you're worn out. In the morning you'll feel better and more cheerful. I'm sorry your happy evening has been spoilt."

He kissed her and went away, and Drina was in bed and pretending to be asleep when her grandmother came in.

In the morning, instead of feeling better, she had a headache and what seemed to be a great weight on her heart. She ate scarcely any breakfast and escaped as soon as she could. A wide hope suddenly filled her. If she could see Madame and explain, she might be willing to help. Drina did not know her private address, except that she lived at the other side of the town, almost in the country, but she might just possibly be at the Selswick School.

In feverish eagerness Drina snatched her purse and flew to the bus stop. But when she reached the Selswick School the old porter told her that Madame was flying to Paris that very morning and would not be back for about a month.

It was the last straw, and it was all Drina could do not to burst into tears there and then. Old Hobbs was an understanding person, with grandchildren of his own, and he saw that the girl was in great distress, so he said nothing when Drina went away upstairs. The place was deserted, except for cleaners, for the term was over and everyone – staff and pupils – had gone.

Drina wandered from studio to studio and sadly did a few exercises at the *barre*.

It couldn't be true that she would never come back there! Never hear Madame's voice again; never see Joy or Cherry or even Daphne. In that miserable hour Drina would have welcomed the fact that she could see Daphne again, smug expression, unkind tongue and all the rest.

For nearly two years, the Selswick School had been the most important place in her life and now that time was over.

Drina stood at one of the big, high windows and looked down into the somewhat dingy street below. She was going away and it looked at the moment as though she could not be a dancer after all. But she would find a way; she would not give up. What had Jenny said? "You're born to be a dancer!" Well, if that were true, and she felt in her heart that it was, a way would be found. Perhaps not at once, but very soon.

Why? she asked herself suddenly, standing there. Why *should* she be born to dance? How had it happened like that?

She mused all the way back to Beech Road and, hunting out her grandmother where she was sorting things in her bedroom, she asked abruptly:

"Granny, did my mother have a job?"

Mrs Chester looked rather startled.

"Yes, of course she had. Everyone has a job now."

"But what was it?"

"Oh, nothing that would – it was not a job that you'd understand. I'll tell you all about it one day, but not now, please, Drina dear. I'm very busy. Why don't you go and see Jenny? You can tell her that we'll expect her to stay with us. She might even be able to come for a few days in September, when we've settled into the new flat. And you're going to the farm in a few days' time. Don't forget that. You always enjoy it."

Suddenly Drina did want Jenny very badly. Her good sense and astringent comments would surely be a help. So she jumped on to her bicycle and in a very few minutes was with her friend.

Jenny looked surprised to see her tragic face.

"I thought you'd be in the seventh heaven! Last night was almost like being a real ballerina, though I expect Madame would have something to say if she could hear me!"

"We're going away and I'm not going to be able to dance any more!" Drina cried, and then she poured out the whole story, while Jenny listened, indignant and horrified.

"And it will all be dreadful. I shall miss you, and – and – oh, Jenny, I was so sure that I was going to be a dancer."

"It's awful!" Jenny groaned. "I shall miss you, too, even if I can come and stay with you. And as for dancing – it's wicked! I just don't understand. They seem so nice usually –"

"They are. They say it's for my own good and lots of things about a ballet dancer's life being hard and giving no time for ordinary living. I'm sure I shan't *want* to live ordinarily!"

"But it is strange – the way your grandparents mind so much. I wonder if there could be a special reason? More than just not wanting you to overwork."

Drina said eagerly, "Oh, Jenny, I've thought of that only this morning. I don't know why I didn't before. Do you think – just possibly – that my mother was a dancer?"

Jenny did not look so surprised as might have been expected.

"Mother wondered that once, but I said you knew nothing about her and had hardly any photographs. Why don't you ask?"

"I couldn't properly, somehow. I did ask just now if she'd had a job, and Granny said of course, but she couldn't explain now. She sounded very sort of brisk, but she looked strange."

"Well, that might be it. It would explain a lot of things, wouldn't it? Perhaps your mother insisted on being a dancer and was in some awful third-rate company. Perhaps her dying even had something to do with it."

"I don't think it can. She was killed in an accident. Granny did tell me that once."

"What kind of accident? And wasn't your father with her?"

"I don't know, and he couldn't have been, because he was dead already."

"Well, perhaps you'll find out more in time. It's silly not to know about your own mother. And do cheer up, because I'm sure you'll be able to dance again somehow."

"Granny says not, but I really think I will — *somehow*." And Drina did cheer up for a time. But as soon as she had left Jenny and was walking under the summer trees in Beech Road her depression returned.

Everything was over. In some ways, it was rather like dying. But there was a sturdy streak in Drina and she returned to her old habit of talking to herself.

"Don't be an idiot, Andrina Adamo! Of course you'll dance. And there'll be lots of ballet to watch in London, perhaps."

She lifted her head up and walked on, slightly comforted.

# BOOK TWO
## Dance to your Shadow

# 1

# Drina in London

For days, Drina ate little and looked so very pale and wretched that her grandmother was much more gentle than usual and really went out of her way, in spite of the fact that she was very busy, to provide her with amusements.

But she was glad, and so was Drina, when it was time for her to go to the farm with Jenny. She went off in low spirits, but she had not been at the farm for an hour before she felt somewhat better. There were new animals to see, including a delightful colt in the River Meadow, and the corn harvest had just started.

She grew very brown and began to eat hungrily, and for the most part she was quite cheerful. But then she would remember sharply that they were not just ordinary holidays. She would never go back to Elleray or the Selswick School, and the knowledge would make her droop again. Jenny always knew and was secretly very upset by her friend's troubles, but she was envious about London in lots of ways.

"I wouldn't like it myself – not for long. But it *will* be fun for you! Think of seeing the Houses of Parliament every day of your life, and the River Thames, and the Tower too."

"The Tower's a long way from the flat," said Drina,

who had been studying, in a desultory way, a map provided by her grandfather.

"Yes, but you can be there in no time on the Tube, or even by river-bus. I'm sure there *are* boats. And you could go to things like Horticultural Shows and Agricultural –"

Drina laughed.

"Oh, Jenny, you know I never would! But I want to go to the theatre. Only Granny will never, never take me to see any ballet. I know she wants me to forget."

"Well, soon you can go by yourself. Why not? You could go to matinées on Saturday afternoons. What's to stop you if you save up the money?"

One evening, Jenny's parents arrived to spend a weekend at the farm, and the next day they took the two girls to Stratford to see *As You Like It* at the Memorial Theatre. Drina enjoyed it and was glad to be inside a theatre again, though she had to stop herself thinking that she might now never have a chance of appearing on a real stage, smelling the theatre smell from the other side of the curtain. Not that the Shakespeare Memorial Theatre actually smelt at all, unlike the shabby, draughty old Grand.

When Drina returned home, leaving Jenny at the farm, she would only have two days there and then they would be moving. She parted from Jenny sadly, for it seemed to her that it might be the end of their friendship. But Jenny had other ideas.

"Now don't forget. We're going to write to each other every week, and sometimes when I'm well off I shall phone you, just so that we can hear the sound of each other's voices. And we'll often stay with each other, too. Why! I'm actually coming up for three days before I go back to school!"

"Yes," said Drina, a little comforted.

She was back in time to pack up her own possessions, and she was standing by her open trunk with several pairs of ballet shoes in her arms when her grandmother found her.

Mrs Chester took in the situation at a glance.

"Now, Drina dear, do hurry up. There's so much to do and it won't help you to moon over your dancing shoes. I think you'd better give them away to someone, One pair of shoes is quite new and there are your practice clothes and all the rest. Why don't you run along to that little girl, Joy Kelly, with them? She may be glad of them, and I believe she's home again now. I know her mother by sight and I saw her this morning."

But Drina looked so tragic that her grandmother said more gently, "Well, you know you won't need them, dear, and they might as well be useful to someone else. But still, if you feel like that, put them all at the bottom of your trunk. You'll soon grow out of them, anyway, though I must say you don't seem to shoot up very fast."

They were tragic words to Drina in her impressionable mood. Yes, she would grow out of them, and when would she ever get new ones? But it was true that, so far, she was not growing very fast and there was plenty of room in the ballet shoes and clothes yet.

Then came the day of the move. The vans came early to take the furniture that was going to the flat and the rest had already been sold. Drina stood sadly in her denuded little room, but was called away by her grandfather. He was anxious to start on the drive to London.

Drina had only been to London twice in her life – or rather in the life that she remembered – and under ordinary circumstances she would have been thrilled when, at last, the seemingly endless suburbs were left behind. It was a hot, sunny day in late August and the trees in Hyde Park looked rather brown, but it made a cheerful scene, with people walking about in bright clothes and half-naked children playing cheerfully.

She caught glimpses of a dozen half-familiar buildings and then they were in Westminster and she saw the towers of the Abbey and the Houses of Parliament.

The entrance to the flats was in a narrow, cool street just off Millbank and Drina was suddenly rather dismayed. It seemed so very dark and closed in, but when they had gone up in the lift, and her grandfather had opened a front door with a key, she ran forward eagerly enough. For there were some small, dusty gardens, a glimpse of the Houses of Parliament, and the wide grey ribbon of the Thames, with a string of barges just emerging from under Lambeth Bridge.

Her own little room had the same view and she felt obscurely that the changing scene on the river might be some comfort. And she really needed comfort during the next day or two, for, though she and her grandmother were very busy settling into the flat, she kept on remembering that her old life was almost entirely over. She tried not to think of Madame and her old friends, but sometimes misery swept over her in a frightening wave.

Her room looked more familiar when her furniture was arranged to her liking and her pictures were up, but nevertheless the pictures hanging on the pale yellow walls gave her another stab of pain. A photograph of the Royal Ballet Company dancing the first act of *Giselle* hung over the fitted electric fire, and there were pictures of Jenny and one of herself, wearing tights and a tutu, that had been taken on one of the occasions when a photographer visited the Selswick School.

She hid her ballet shoes and practice clothes at the back of a cupboard, and then changed her mind and took one pair of shoes out again, putting them in a more handy place. For the unexpectedly large bathroom held a very solid and conveniently placed towel-rail and she meant to keep up her practising as best she could every day. For though one part of her mind believed that her grandmother meant what she said and she was finished with dancing, another and far more vigorous part knew that she *must* dance again, even if not just yet.

Once they were more or less settled, Mr Chester planned to take Drina about London for a few days, for he was not starting his new job until the middle of the following week.

It was strange to be in Westminster, with the sound of the bells and the deep tones of Big Ben so often in her ears, and there were times during the first day or two when Drina really thought that she must be dreaming. She told herself that she would wake up and find herself back in Beech Road, hurrying on her way to see Jenny.

Mr Chester provided Drina not only with several clever little pictorial maps of London, but with a detailed street map and a plan of the Tubes, and he let her choose their first excursions. Together they walked along the Embankment towards Waterloo Bridge in the bright sunshine, and he pointed out famous landmarks and expected her to remember their exact locality. They walked across St James's Park, saw the Changing of the Guard at Buckingham Palace, and then went up Constitution Hill to Hyde Park Corner and into the maze of Mayfair streets beyond. Drina was fascinated by the attractive little painted houses in many a hidden mews and by the reality of being in Berkeley and

Grosvenor Squares.

They went to the Tower and the Zoo and, on a wet day, to Madame Tussaud's, and out to Highgate, where they walked to Kenwood House and afterwards over Hampstead Heath.

During these outings Drina was almost happy, for the sun shone most of the time and it was really exciting to feel that she was getting to know London. They made a sort of game of finding their way about and she was an apt pupil in learning her way from one place to another. Soon she had a pretty good idea of the Tubes and could recite strings of stations on the different lines. She knew where the most famous shops were and visited some of them with her grandmother. Harrods she loved, especially the book department.

As they went about London she looked often for indications that there was some ballet either on or about to be on. But just then there was nothing and she was almost relieved. It would have been awful to see it advertised and then not to be allowed to go.

Drina's new school was called the Pakington School and was in a street off Grosvenor Place. Her grandmother took her there one day to meet the headmistress and see over the building, which was two large houses knocked into one. There were two imposing pillared front entrances and a glimpse from the front windows, up the street and across the main road, of the gardens of Buckingham palace.

The headmistress was pleasant enough, but Drina found that she was almost dreading the time when she must start anew amongst strange girls, in an atmosphere that must surely be very different from Elleray School.

"You'll find all sorts of different ways of going to school," her grandfather said cheerfully one evening. "You can vary it according to your mood. You can ge the bus along Victoria Street to Victoria Station, or Birdcage Walk and past the Palace. I can see you'll soor be an out-and-out little Londoner! Only don't speak to strangers, Drina, and —"

"Not unless they ask the way!" said Drina, with a giggle. She had twice that day been asked the way by bewildered-looking people and had been proud to be able to direct them correctly.

"Well, you must use your common sense, of course. But do be careful. London is very different from Willerbury."

But the first newness and excitement soon wore off, Mr Chester began to leave for the office every morning and Drina's spirits drooped again. She was pale anc listless and had little appetite, and she began to spenc a good deal of time reading in Victoria Tower Gardens, beside the Houses of Parliament.

Mrs Chester was privately very worried, but she said nothing, merely arranging what outings she could. The new school uniform had to be bought and everything marked, but Drina hated sewing and was not cheered at having to sew name-tapes on her new blazer, coat, raincoat, shoebag and other possessions.

Jenny wrote almost every day and Drina looked forward to the arrival of the post, for Jenny was a chatty correspondent and her news was always lively and amusing. In her turn, Drina wrote long letters to her friend, lying on her stomach on the parched grass in Victoria Tower Gardens, with the sounds of the river and the London traffic in her ears. But it was not as good as actually being with Jenny and Drina looked forward keenly to her friend's short visit.

The day came at last when Jenny was due to arrive, and Drina and her grandmother went to Paddington to meet the train. Jenny was patently in high spirits when she ran past the barrier and her presence immediately cheered Drina up. But that night when they were undressing together, though Jenny was actually to sleep in the small spare room, Drina told her friend just how she felt, which was a great relief. She had tried in her letters, but it was not so easy as telling Jenny face to face.

"They've been lovely, both of them, but sometimes I feel most terribly miserable. I practice every day in the bathroom, and I'm *sure* that I'll get the chance to dance again, but I don't know how to wait. Oh, Jenny!"

"It's horrible for you!" said Jenny, with real sympathy. "And Madame thinks so, too. I met her in town the other day and she didn't say much, but I gathered she was really upset at losing you and to hear that you've had to give up dancing. Your grandmother always seems really nice, but over this I do think she's cruel. By the way, I think Madame wrote to her and told her that she thought you ought to dance."

"Granny didn't tell me that, and she doesn't mean to be cruel," Drina said fairly but drearily. "She really thinks that dancing's bad for me. And she keeps on talking about what fun it will be in London at Christmas and how I'll like school. I shan't like it a bit, or that's how I feel now. There won't be anyone like you at the Pakington, I'm quite sure. Do you remember how you banged into me that first day and started talking about ballet?"

"I've got a lot to answer for," said Jenny, quite seriously. "You'd never have gone to Madame but for me, and then you wouldn't be miserable now."

"I think I would have gone to her somehow. It wasn't only you. I wanted to dance."

"And you will. I *know* you will! You couldn't not. So do cheer up."

And Drina did cheer up again for the three days that Jenny was with her. Then, immediately she had waved her friend away at Paddington, unhappiness descended on her again. That night she heard a song on the radio and the words suddenly struck home.

"Dance to your shadow when there's nothing better
    near you –"

"Dance to your shadow!" Drina thought. "Oh, dear! I am! There's nothing else to dance to." And she found that the half-heard words of the Hebridean song haunted her.

Mrs Chester tried being extra brisk and cheerful, which was *not* the treatment that Drina needed just then, and both were glad, on the whole, when the time came for Drina to go to her new school. It would mean that at least she was occupied for a good part of each day.

# 2

# Ballet Books
# and a Stranger

Mrs Chester had offered to go with Drina to school that first morning, but she firmly refused the offer. The years at Elleray and the Selswick School had made her very independent and, though she was not really looking forward at all to meeting so many new people, she was not shy. At the Selswick, she had got used to meeting all kinds and ages of students and she had been popular at Elleray, a fact which had given her confidence.

It was a bright September morning and she left early and was passing Buckingham Palace not very long after half-past eight. She stared at its impressive frontage and then back up the wide, tree-lined Mall and, as it had done often before, a feeling of disbelief flooded her. It was so *odd* to be in London; so very strange and unlikely to be going to school past the Palace and up Buckingham Palace Road.

Her new uniform was very smart and suited her, for it was dark red and pale blue. She no longer carried a school-bag, as she had done on that first occasion at Elleray School, but now had a neat little case with her initials on it.

She walked more and more slowly as she entered the school gates, but the girls who went past her wearing the same uniform took little notice of her. They were mostly much older and she knew already that the youngest girls would be her own age, eleven. Though, as she would soon be twelve, she had been placed in Class 2.

Her arrival was in no way like that earlier arrival at Elleray School, for she entered the right hand door alone and was directed to the cloakrooms by a brisk young teacher, who took her name and asked her to come back to her when she had removed her outdoor clothes and changed her shoes.

There was no one in the junior cloakroom who struck Drina as being in the least like Jenny. Nearly all the girls seemed to be too occupied with holiday chatter to bother about her, though one or two smiled and one pointed out an empty peg. They had clear, confident, rather unfamiliar voices and the talk was mostly about holidays abroad.

Drina listened with some interest, trying to note a few faces for future reference, but she changed her shoes in silence, combed her thick hair and then returned as told to the entrance hall, where the young teacher had by then gathered half a dozen more new girls, most of them looking shyer than Drina, but not, she thought pessimistically, especially interesting.

There was a fat girl who kept on wiping a rather pink nose nervously, twins who seemed only to want to talk to each other, a foreign child who seemed to know very little English, and two girls of quite fifteen.

The fat girl muttered to Drina, "Hey! How old are you? I thought they didn't take girls under eleven."

"I shall be twelve next month," Drina informed her with dignity, though she did not normally mind her smallness.

The fat one gave another nervous dab at her nose

and seemed to lose interest, and Drina thought with passionate longing of Elleray School, returning on the same day, and of Jenny standing in their usual place in hall. Why, oh why had life dumped her in this London school?

After assembly, Drina's class gathered in one of the big front classrooms. Somehow she found herself in possession of a desk by the window and was a little comforted to have an attractive glimpse across the busy main road of the gardens of the Palace.

Just in front of her were three girls who looked pleasant and merry; all fair and rather alike, though they could hardly be sisters, unless, of course, they were triplets. They seemed to be called Jane, Barbara and Belinda and each separately turned round and grinned at Drina, which was cheering, though she had no chance to talk to them until Break. Only the higher classes, it appeared, walked in the garden on fine days, and the younger ones gathered in groups indoors. Later Drina learned that the garden was very small, because a gym. with quite a large stage had been built out from the main structure.

Now the talk seemed to be more about horse riding than anything else, though there was one little group passionately discussing ice skating. Drina, standing a little apart, listened and observed and wondered if anywhere amongst so many girls there was someone who would turn into a special friend.

One girl interested and curiously repelled her. She was sitting perched on a table, almost as though she were holding court. She had curly black hair and green eyes and seemed very pleased with herself. She was handsome and confident, but her face was by no means lovable and her laugh was too loud.

"Looking at the beautiful Candida?" a voice asked at

her elbow and she found the fair girl called Barbara standing there with her two friends.

"I don't know anyone yet," said Drina, pleased to see them.

"Oh, you soon will. But Candida Selcourt is in 3A, you know. We don't much care for her, but she has quite a following. What's *your* name?"

"Andrina Adamo," said Drina. "But I'm usually called Drina Adams."

"Oh, wow! What a strange name! No wonder you change it to Adams. Are you foreign? We get quite a lot of foreigners."

"Not really, though my father was Italian," Drina explained.

"Yes, you look sort of Italian. Where do you live?"

"In Westminster. We've got a flat near the river. We've only just come to London from – from Warwickshire."

"How strange for you! But I expect you'll like it. Do you ride or ice skate?"

Drina shook her head, so that her hair flew out.

"No, though Granny often says I should learn."

"Oh, you'll have to. Everyone's crazy on riding and skating here. What *do* you do?"

Drina hesitated.

"I used to dance, but I'm not learning at the moment."

"Dance? What kind?"

"Ballet," said Drina, watching their faces.

But the three remained comparatively unresponsive.

"Oh!"

"Doesn't *anyone* learn ballet?"

"Oh, some may do," said Belinda, rather vaguely. "I know that quite a few learn tap dancing or Greek. The only one we *know* learns ballet is Candida."

Somehow Drina was not surprised to hear that, though the information did not make her long to be friends with the showy Candida.

"She goes to some Ballet School or other and is going to be a ballerina, or so she says. She's always talking about it. She talks altogether too much about herself."

"Oh!" said Drina in her turn, and then the bell rang and they streamed back up the broad staircase back to their classroom.

There was a two-hour break in the middle of the day and Drina returned to the flat by bus. Her grandmother asked a number of interested questions and she did her best to answer them, though she did not embroider her replies. Yes, the school seemed quite pleasant. Yes, there were some nice girls in her class, especially three who sat near her. Yes, she had enjoyed her morning.

Mrs Chester sighed and watched her set off again, noting the slight droop of the usually well held shoulders. It was so unlike Drina to slouch. But surely, after a few days at school, she would find new interests and make new friends? It was what they both hoped for most fervently for their grandchild.

After a week, Drina was fairly well at home at the Pakington School and she knew something about most of the girls in her class. She was well on the way to being friends with Jane, Barbara and Belinda and was enjoying the work, which was interesting and varied. She continued to like the journey to school and there were moments when she was stabbed sharply by the fascination of London. When the bells of Westminster suddenly pealed out, when she caught glimpses of the Mall and the buildings of Whitehall through the trees of St James's Park, her heart would lift in sudden pleasure and excitement.

She did not always hurry home from school, for there was so much to see. Sometimes she lingered by the lake in the park, watching the water-fowl, and on a few occasions she slipped into the continental part of Victoria Station to see the afternoon Boat Train depart. It was thrilling, she found, to watch lucky people departing for the continent and to see the labels on their luggage. It brought places that she had never seen – Calais, Paris, Basle, Rome – a good deal nearer, somehow, and she always drew in her breath sharply when the long train started on its non-stop run to the coast.

But she never confessed about her visits to Victoria to the rather sophisticated trio who were beginning to be, in a mild way, her friends. *They*, though only twelve, had all been abroad several times, and they could talk knowledgeably about the Alps, the French Riviera and Paris. They had not spent most of their lives in a town in the Midlands, giving most of their heart and attention to learning to dance. Drina, who had only been to Wales and Scotland, felt at a disadvantage and, in some ways, envied them very much.

They did not understand her lost, absorbing world and she rarely spoke of it. Only to Jenny in her long letters did she confess about her continuing solitary practices in the bathroom and her wistfulness when she heard ballet music on the radio. She felt oddly unattached and remote, not yet having found a complete new world and not really wanting to do so. She wanted to *dance* with the same need that she had always wanted it.

She did not get to know Candida, though on several occasions she overheard her talking about the Ballet School, which was one Drina herself had never heard about. Furthermore, it appeared that Candida was to dance in the Pakington School Christmas play, which had been cast at the end of the summer term, though actual rehearsals did not start until a week or two after the beginning of the autumn term.

Drina did not expect a part, but was told one day that she could be in the crowd scenes. She went to the first rehearsal as ordered and found it quite curious to watch a play, rather than a ballet, beginning to take shape. The Pakington School had a high standard and believed in putting on only well rehearsed shows and the stage manager was the vigorous, intelligent young teacher she had met that first day in the hall.

It was an interesting play, based on a Scandinavian folk tale. There were to be several little songs in it, but just the once dance, by Candida Selcourt, who was supposed to be a black swan.

"Thinks she's Pavlova at the very least!" Barbara said in Drina's ear, but Drina was not even listening. She was watching Candida with great attention and watching her, strangely, almost with Madame's eyes. Candida was certainly a showy dancer and had obviously been learning for some time, but she had certain faults of technique that Drina spotted at once. She could hear Madame's caustic voice and almost felt herself back at the Selswick School.

But Candida seemed unaware that there were any faults, and apparently no one else was in a position to judge. It was generally accepted by the staff that Candida danced very nicely and that her performance would add greatly to the success of the play.

Early in October Drina joined a public library and the moment her homework was finished in the evenings she would settle down to read. She soon ran the ballet books to earth in the non-fiction corner and began to work steadily through them. She still read ballet stories occasionally, but now it was the books that told the history of the ballet and about the well-known dancers of the past and present that really drew her.

She read about many ballets that she had never seen, about the Russian School, and about many of the great male and female dancers: Massine, Dolin, Pavlova, Markova, Fonteyn, Ivory. She pored over the many pictures and did her best to visualise what some of the famous ballets would look like on the stage. Most of all she was interested to read about the ballet called *The Breton Wedding*. It was a ballet that had been made for Elizabeth Ivory and she had had her greatest success in the role of the tragic fishergirl, Josette. After her early and sudden death, explained one writer, the ballet had never been revived, and there was a legend in the ballet world that it would not be danced again for twenty years. Some dancers had got the idea that it was unlucky and it had never been included in any repertoire.

As well as the library, there were the bookshops and Drina took to looking out for new ballet books and browsing over them. There was one shop in Victoria

Street of which she was particularly fond and the proprietor never seemed to mind how long she lingered there, with her nose in a ballet book. In fact, he sometimes pointed out new ones and made intelligent comments. He was a ballet enthusiast, it seemed, and always went to the opening of the season at the Royal Opera House, Covent Garden, and to as many other performances as he could manage.

One day, Drina dropped in on her way from school and was soon absorbed in a new book, mainly of beautiful pictures. She stared at the one of *The Breton Wedding* for a long time, for it was in colour, and for the first time she could really get the effect of the blue nets of the fishermen overhanging the narrow little street of uneven small houses. In the centre was Elizabeth Ivory as Josette, her lovely body graceful in an arabesque.

"She looks so happy there," Drina thought. "That must be in the first act when she's just married her fisherman. Or perhaps just before she marries him; I don't really know. I know it all takes place at the time of the Blessing of the Nets, and then her husband goes away with the tunny-fishers and is drowned in a great storm."

"That's a wonderful picture!" said a female voice suddenly at her elbow and Drina starting violently, found herself looking up into an attractive face. The woman was not very young, but she was smartly dressed and almost beautiful.

"I wish I could have seen it," said Drina, still holding the book.

"Well, you couldn't, of course. Ivory died a number of years ago. Actually I was there that last night when Ivory danced Josette. Twenty-four hours later she was dead."

"Oh!" Drina put down the book in its place and stared eagerly at the stranger. "Were you really? I knew she had a tragic death; all the books say so. But not one of the ones that I've read has said just what happened. They talk more about the roles that she created."

"She was flying to the States to be a guest artist in New York. The plane crashed and all the passengers were killed. Ivory was only twenty-five and had years of dancing before her. I agree with the people who think she was the greatest of them all." Then she smiled and walked away, rather slowly. Drina noticed that she had a slight limp.

"She used to be a dancer," said the proprietor, noticing Drina's interest. "She was with the Igor Dominick Company —"

"But so was Ivory!"

"Yes. This Miss Whiteway was dancing in that ballet on the night she was speaking about. She was only in the *corps de ballet* then, I believe, but she was regarded as having great promise. She had some sort of accident soon after she had danced her first ballerina roles and was left with a limp. A tragedy, really!"

"Oh, yes!" agreed Drina, horrified.

"She often comes in here and buys ballet books."

Drina hurried home then, her mind filled with thoughts of Elizabeth Ivory's tragic death, and with the little she had learned of Miss Whiteway. Somehow the story was such that it helped her a good deal.

How feeble it was of her to suffer so much because she could not dance for a little while! It must be so much worse to know that, for physical reasons, you could never dance again.

It would, thought Drina, take more courage than she possessed to bear a thing like that.

# 3

# In the Fog

By the time October was going on its way, Drina had almost forgotten summer. It seemed almost in another life that she and Jenny had worked and lazed on the farm, helping with the harvest, feeding the hens, and wandering through the rich Warwickshire fields and the cool woodland. The last traces of her tan had long since faded and she was very pale, even paler than she had been during the winters at Willerbury.

Mrs Chester sometimes wondered anxiously if London suited her. The child was still, at times, very listless, and a good deal of her joy in life seemed to have been quenched.

"We ought to let her have ballet lessons again," said Mr Chester one night, when Drina was in bed.

His wife looked at him with raised eyebrows.

"My dear James! We agreed that dancing wasn't good for her and she must learn to forget about it. After a year or two, when she has had plenty of other interests, we can suggest lessons in ballroom dancing. She moves beautifully already."

"Of course she does. She moves like a born dancer, and you know it," said her husband, staring at her over his paper. "And she strikes me as being the kind of child who never will forget the things she cares about.

She takes after her mother."

"Well, I've done my best," said Mrs Chester, very abruptly. "And it's all for Drina's good, though she doesn't realise it now, perhaps."

"No, I don't think she does realise it. Do you know that she reads nothing but books about the ballet?"

"I saw she had some in her room. I'd like to forbid it, but I suppose I can't quite do that."

"No. It wouldn't do any good. Well, my dear, you know your own mind, too, but I hope we're doing right."

"Of course we're doing right. And Drina seems to be doing well at school. Making friends as well. I like those three girls who came to tea, and she's visited them in their homes. Christmas will be a help, too. She'll love to see the decorations and we must take her to several shows and the Christmas morning service in the Abbey. She can't be such an unnatural girl that she won't enjoy it all?"

Mr Chester said no more, for he knew his wife's determination, but he did not fail to note the continual arrival of the ballet books and Drina's expression when she heard ballet music on the radio one evening.

But Drina never mentioned dancing to her grandparents and really was honestly trying to settle down in her new life. Some things she genuinely enjoyed. She was taking London to her heart and was constantly entranced by the changing aspects of the city. She loved the wintry park and the blue haze that settled over the Mall in the late afternoon. She loved the brilliantly loaded barrows of the street traders, the sight of so many interesting foreigners in the streets, the sound of the river traffic. The bells of Westminster already seemed part of her life, and in some ways, looking back, Willerbury seemed to have been very dull. Or it would have been dull but for Jenny and the Selswick School.

She still heard from Jenny regularly, and Joy Kelly wrote, too, telling her all the gossip from the Selswick. They were doing a new ballet for the Christmas Show and Daphne was disgusted because she had not got a good part. But she was not improving rapidly enough to please Madame. Old Hobbs had had rheumatism and had been away for a week; the heating system had failed for three whole days and they had all shivered as they danced; several of the older girls were going to have auditions for the Christmas pantomime at the Grand. Madame had suggested that Cherry, Mark Playford and Joy herself should go also, as they were all just old enough. Drina read the news with wistful interest and then burned the letters. But while she read she could see the Selswick School, Madame, Daphne and all the others.

Then, almost at the end of October, something happened that altered her life a certain amount and provided her with a problem.

At lunch-time one Monday, her grandmother said, "I'm going out to Swiss Cottage this afternoon to have tea with an old school friend of mine, Drina. I shan't be back till about six o'clock and your grandfather isn't expected until late. Will you be all right? Can you get your own tea if I leave it more or less ready?"

"Oh, yes, Granny," Drina said willingly enough. "I'll be quite all right."

"Well, go down to Mrs Willis if you're lonely. You know she'd be glad to have you. She's a most motherly woman." Mrs Willis had a flat on the floor below.

"Oh, yes, I will, but I shan't be lonely. I'll get on with my homework."

When Drina left school at four o'clock it was rather

foggy, but not enough to be alarming. She was supposed to take a taxi, but she had received two book tokens for her birthday and was anxious to exchange them, so she decided to go home along Victoria Street and visit her favourite bookshop. She spent a long time choosing her books and would not have left then if Mr Bird, the proprietor, had not pointed out that the fog was getting thicker.

"It'll be worse nearer the river, too. You'd really better hurry home."

So the books were parcelled up and Drina did try to get a taxi, but with no luck. So she set out to walk, rather thrilled by the heavy yellow pall that was beginning to hide the buildings. The lights were on in the shops and traffic was only crawling past. It really was quite exciting to be out in a real fog!

She was by then fairly used to the short cuts through the streets behind the Abbey and she would have said that she knew her way well. But the fog was certainly thicker as she neared the river, so thick, in fact, that it made her cough and her eyes water. Presently she could scarcely see a yard in front of her and the experience began to be more frightening than interesting.

It was very cold indeed and her teeth began to chatter; the few people who passed her almost silently looked like ghosts. A large black cat startled her very much and took her attention from the street she was just about to cross. She was halfway over the road when a car nosed its way almost on top of her and she leaped for where she thought the pavement must be. Her toes caught on the edge and she fell awkwardly, dropping her books and case and hitting her elbow against a lamp standard. The pain was so sharp, even through her thick coat, that she felt almost sick

for a moment.

She groped for her parcel and case and stood there dazedly, wondering where on earth she could be. Somewhere in the fog Big Ben struck five o'clock, but though she tried to take her direction from the sound it was almost like being blind.

She was extremely relieved when someone came towards her along the pavement and she began to stammer a little incoherently as soon as the woman was level with her.

"Excuse me, but – I don't know where I am! I want to get to –" And she named the street where the block of flats was.

"You poor child!" said a strangely familiar voice. "You do look lost! What's the matter? It isn't only the fog, is it? Aren't you well?"

"I – I fell," Said Drina, rather breathlessly, "and banged my arm. A car nearly knocked me down and –" And then, as she peered up into the stranger's face, she cried, "Why! You're Miss Whiteway! Mr Bird told me your name."

"Mr Bird? Oh, in the bookshop? Now I come to think of it I've seen you before. Aren't you the little girl who was looking at the ballet books?"

"Yes," said Drina, much relieved.

"Well, I only live just along here. I've been to the post and it isn't more than ten yards to my front door. Would you like to come in and get warm? We'll make a cup of tea and then I'll take you home. I can find my way even in a fog as thick as this. But will anyone be worrying about you? Because if they will I'll telephone."

"No. Granny's out. She's gone to see a friend at Swiss Cottage. Unless she got worried about the fog and came home earlier."

"It may not be bad out there. Will you come, then? You're cold to the bone."

Drina hesitated. Her grandparents had repeatedly warned her against strangers, but Miss Whiteway seemed so very charming and Mr Bird, had seemed to know about her. Besides, she had once belonged to the world of ballet and the thought drew Drina strongly.

Miss Whiteway seemed to read her thoughts.

"You're wondering if you ought to visit a stranger? But it will only be for a few minutes and if you're really interested in ballet books I've got a fine collection."

That settled it, of course, and Drina trotted thankfully at her side. In a moment or two, they came to a blue-painted doorway reached by a flight of steps. There was a series of bells, each with a card attached.

"Mine's the bottom flat," said Miss Whiteway, leading the way into the entrance hall. "Just wait while I fish out my key."

She had soon opened her door and was ushering Drina along a small, narrow hall and into a very attractive living-room.

"The kettle's on already. I'll just make the tea. But first slip off your coat and let me look at your arm. Is it hurting much?"

"It's getting better now," said Drina, but she winced as she took off her coat and rolled up the sleeve of her dark red sweater. A bruise was already coming up on her white skin.

"You *must* have given it a bang! I'll put something on it for you. And goodness! Your hands are icy! Would you like to hold them under the hot tap? The bathroom's the second door on the left."

Drina went out into the little hall again and, perhaps because she was still rather dazed, opened the first door on the left. At what she saw she stared blankly, for the room was a small bare studio, with a *barre* fitted along one wall. There was a record player and records and the walls were decorated with photographs of dancers.

She shut the door again hastily and managed to find the bathroom, and when she returned Miss Whiteway had made the tea and was carrying in a small tray.

"Would you like some chocolate biscuits with it?"

"Yes, please!" Drina was hungry after her long afternoon. Then she added shyly, "I'm so sorry, but I opened the wrong door. You – you've got a studio, but I – I thought –"

Miss Whiteway had taken off her coat and she wore

a well-cut black dress. Her hair was brown and wavy and her body still beautiful, though the slight limp marred her walk. Her face, even to Drina's eyes, had great character and was enhanced rather than spoilt by the lines of past suffering.

"Yes. My niece lives with me. She goes to the Igor Dominick School here in London. They've got a boarding-school in the country, too, but her parents prefer her to be with me. She practices here. What did you think?"

Drina blushed vividly, feeling that she had been tactless. She stammered, "Mr Bird said – he told me – that you used to dance."

"Oh, yes," Miss Whiteway agreed easily. "I was a dancer until my accident, when I damaged my foot. Now I design the sets for new ballets, mainly for the Igor Dominick productions. You know they've got a theatre and company of their own, I expect?"

"Oh, yes," said Drina eagerly. She knew all about the Royal Ballet Company and Covent Garden, and the Igor Dominick Theatre on the Embankment near Waterloo Bridge.

"My niece is thirteen and her name's Lena. I believe they think quite well of her at the school, but for myself I'm not convinced yet that she'll make a really good dancer. Marianne Volonaise says she has talent, but that can mean anything or nothing. It takes more than talent to lift a dancer out of the rut. Do have a biscuit and is your tea how you like it?"

"It's lovely! I feel much better," said Drina gratefully, taking a chocolate biscuit and biting it hungrily.

"You've got rather the look of a dancer yourself. I noticed it in the shop. You hold your head well and your back is strong and straight. *Are* you a dancer?"

Drina stared back at her, suddenly conscious that she

did not want to explain that she might now never have the chance of being a dancer. It was more than that; for some reason she *could* not tell her.

"I – I learned from Madame – Miss Selswick – for nearly two years."

"Janetta Selswick? Well, she's a first-rate teacher. She's sent plenty of good dancers to London from that remote town in the Midlands where she has her school. But are you living in London now?"

"Yes. We – we moved in August. I haven't got a father and mother and I live with my grandparents."

"You know my name, but I haven't heard yours," said Miss Whiteway, smiling warmly at her.

"Drina Adams." Again Drina was surprised at herself. *Why* didn't she want to give her full name? Perhaps it was because Andrina Adamo, who had danced Snow White at the Summer Show, seemed so incredibly far away, almost another person.

"Well, tell me, Drina. From whom are you learning now? I see that you go the Pakington School, but you'll learn no dancing there!"

"No," said Drina. "The girls mostly only care about riding and skating and we don't do any dancing in class, even. I – I'm not learning at all just now. Granny said she wanted me to – to find other interests for a time. But – but I expect she'll arrange something soon. I practise in the bathroom. There's a very good towel-rail," she added naively.

Miss Whiteway laughed.

"And you're really interested?"

"More than anything else in the world."

Miss Whiteway was silent for some time, then she said abruptly, "Bathrooms are all very well, but a dancer should have space. I wonder if you'd like to practise here? I could write and introduce myself to your grandmother. She may think it very strange, of course, but I'm extremely respectable! My uncle is Canon Whiteway at the Abbey. She could telephone to him if she'd like a reference. I do love having young dancers under my eyes and Lena would like to think of someone else using her *barre*. You'd meet her, of course, sometimes. Lena and Drina! You certainly ought to be friends."

Drina was quite carried away. She had forgotten cold and fog and her aching elbow.

"It's very kind of you! I'd like it very, very much. But wouldn't it be a nuisance?"

"Not the slightest nuisance. We could arrange a time, couldn't we? I'd be glad to help a pupil of Janetta's. We knew each other once."

"*Did* you? But – but I thought that Miss Selswick was with the Royal Ballet."

"Oh, yes, but she wasn't always with them. We were together once, when we were both very young. That was before I joined the Igor Dominick Company. I'd only been in that a very few months when Ivory died. Well, I'll write the note to your grandmother and give her the Canon's telephone number. It may be rather unconventional, our meeting in a bookshop and in a fog, but perhaps she won't mind."

Drina was too happy to think much about it then, but when Miss Whiteway had left her at the entrance to her own home, and she was moving upwards in the lift, she suddenly realised just what she had done.

Was there even the barest of chances that her grandmother would let her take advantage of Miss Whiteway's offer?

She got out of the lift and walked towards the door of the flat with a heavy heart.

# 4

# Drina's Double
# Life

The flat was dark and deserted. Drina turned on the lights and dropped on to the rug to think, ignoring her tea, which was spread on the end of the table. In a while she might be hungry, in spite of tea and chocolate biscuits, but she had to think while she had the chance.

What was she to do? If she explained about her meetings with Miss Whiteway and produced the note, her grandmother would almost certainly forbid the new friendship. She would certainly never agree to letting Drina go there to practise when she thought that no practising was necessary.

What about appealing to her grandfather then? But what good would that do? It had definitely been decided that she was not to dance, so the natural reply to her pleadings would be that she did not need to practise.

Yet Drina thought with more and more eagerness and wistfulness of the little studio, the rows of ballet books in the many bookcases in Miss Whiteway's sitting-room, and of Miss Whiteway herself – Adele Whiteway, she had said her full name was – and her lost career as a ballet dancer. She had expected her to be a tragic person, soured by the premature ending of her life as a dancer, but it was evident that she had made a new life for herself. She designed the sets for new ballets and she helped young dancers.

"Not a bit sorry for herself!" thought Drina with admiration. It was the first time she had ever realised that a dreadful happening could lead to something else; something perhaps not so exciting, but as creative in its own way.

It would be desperately hard to have to give up Miss Whiteway when she was only just beginning to know her, and harder still to lose that wonderful chance of a real place to practise in, with someone knowledgeable to help and advise. But what else could she do?

Drina was normally an exceedingly honest girl. She had rarely deliberately deceived her grandmother, except on that long-ago occasion when she had gone with Jenny to watch the ballet class, and even then she had tried to confess. Of course, her continued practices were a deception in a way, but they seemed entirely justified to her, believing as she still did that some day her grandmother would change her mind about ballet lessons.

But would she change it now? It seemed unlikely.

Drina took Miss Whiteway's note from her case and stared at it for a long time, and then suddenly, with a rather desperate gesture, she tore it into little pieces. It was no use. She could *not* show it to her grandmother and watch her face take on that withdrawn, disapproving expression.

She dropped the pieces into the wastepaper basket and knew even then what she would do. It would be very wrong, she supposed, but she was going to tell Miss Whiteway that it was all right and she was

somehow going to smuggle her practice clothes and shoes out of the flat. She would ask Miss Whiteway if she could practise every day after school. She could perhaps tell her grandmother that she was staying at school for rehearsals of the play, which would be true up to a point. There was a rehearsal three times a week at four o'clock, though the girls with small parts were not always required to be present.

Rather shocked at herself, but very determined, Drina at last rose stiffly from the rug, boiled the kettle and made herself some tea. She sat down at the table and began to eat the homemade meat-pie and salad that her grandmother had left, and was just finishing when a key turned in the front door and her grandmother's voice called anxiously.

"Drina, are you here?"

"Yes, Granny!" she called.

"Thank goodness! I'd no idea the fog was so bad. It seems mostly to be along the river. Oh, you've had your tea? Good girl! Then I suppose you'll be wanting to get on with your homework?"

"I suppose I'd better," said Drina, feeling guilty and sure that her sensations would show on her face. But Mrs Chester merely said:

"Would you sooner do it in here?"

But Drina took her case and retreated to her own little room. She switched on her reading-lamp and settled down at the small table that her grandmother had provided. But all the time, as she strove to deal with Maths, French and Geography, her thoughts were going round and round.

Had she been very wicked? Not only to tear up the note, but to make all those plans that she had every intention of carrying out? Wasn't it a dreadful way to reward her grandparents for all the kindness to her? But she knew, and was more sure by the time she went to bed, that nothing would stop her taking advantage of Miss Whiteway's offer. She could *not* refuse. And surely, when her grandmother found out, as probably she would sooner or later, she would understand? To Drina then it seemed so obvious that she must dance that she even visualised her grandmother's forgiveness and understanding without undue difficulty.

By carrying some of her books she managed to get her practice clothes and one pair of shoes into her case the next morning, and all day she thought of seeing Miss Whiteway again and having a chance to practise properly.

Miss Whiteway received her warmly, but did not waste time. To Drina's relief she seemed to take it for granted that Mrs Chester knew all about the arrangement. Drina felt guiltier than ever, but at least she had not had to lie in words.

"I'm so glad that your grandmother agreed," said Miss Whiteway cheerfully. "I'd like to meet her one of these days and hear what she plans for you. But I won't waste your time. I know you'd like to change and start right away."

She left Drina alone for some time, then knocked at the studio door and entered slowly.

"Would you mind if I watched? I won't always be able to when I'm busy, but I've some free time this afternoon."

She watched in silence while Drina went through her exercises at the *barre*, and her face was very intent. Occasionally, she gave an approving nod.

Finally she said, "I can see that Janetta Selswick has started you well. You have a few of the usual faults and, in fact, all the good points of a prospective dancer. Would you like to do a dance for me? There are some records over there. See if you can find something suitable."

Drina turned the records eagerly and was lucky enough to find the music for one of her Snow White dances.

"I could dance to this! I was Snow White in our Summer Show at the Selswick. But I haven't really danced since the end of July."

"Never mind. You've kept yourself very supple and in excellent practice."

"I ought to have my Snow White dress on. It was so pretty."

"Never mind that, either."

She put on the record while Drina waited, poised. The moment the music started she forgot all about the bare little studio and Miss Whiteway and was back in the small theatre at the Selswick. It was wonderful to dance again! She was so happy that she felt she must have been almost dead for three long months.

"Yes," said Adele Whiteway at the end. "Yes. Well, I can see why Janetta chose you to dance the leading part in her ballet. You ought to go for an audition at the Royal Ballet School or the Dominick one. But I expect your grandmother has that in hand."

Drina said nothing, for she was wondering how long she could keep up the deception. It made her feel worse than she had supposed now that she was not actually dancing. She almost burst out, "She doesn't mean me to dance! I never told her about you!"

But she lost her chance, for Adele Whiteway said briskly, "I expect you ought to run along home. It's almost dark and getting a trifle misty. I won't ask you to stay for a cup of tea. Would you like me to come with you?"

"No, thank you. I shall be quite all right in a taxi," said Drina and hastily changed back into her school clothes.

"Tomorrow then? Look! I'll give you one of my spare keys and you can get in if I should happen to be out. Goodbye, my dear!"

"Goodbye and thank you!" cried Drina and fled. As she ran, Big Ben struck five and she thought how long it seemed since she had heard the same strokes yesterday. So much had happened since then.

By the time a week had passed Drina was almost used to her double life. The feeling of guilt was her constant companion, but mostly she managed to push it well into the background. Her eyes grew bright again and her black hair seemed to take on an extra lustre. She walked with a springy step and held her head well poised on all occasions.

Mrs Chester was delighted, but slightly puzzled.

"It must be that school play. She seems rather keen on it. I only hope, though, that we aren't going to have a stagestruck child on our hands instead of a ballet one!"

"But she only has a walking-on part," said her husband.

"Well, something's changed her and for the better. I suppose the best thing to do now is to let well alone."

As a matter of fact, Drina was quite interested in the play, for she could not help admiring the competent way it was taking shape and the dresses sounded as though they would be very attractive. As a peasant child she was to wear a bright red skirt and a dark green bodice and these Mrs Chester was having made.

Drina was also interested in Candida, though she did not like her much. She had spoken to her a few times now, but Candida was arrogant and not disposed to take much notice of a girl from a lower class who appeared to be quite undistinguished.

With Jane, Barbara and Belinda, Drina was happy in school and she sometimes saw them on Saturdays. They were a nice trio and. being slightly older and much taller, they were inclined to spoil her a little. They admired her looks, which were in great contrast to their own fairness, and included her in most of their fun and plans.

Drina never spoke of her dancing, but, as it happened, they saw her dance one day. It happened because Drina was passing the hall alone and the vast expanse of floor tempted her. There was no one in sight and she slipped out into the centre and began to do her Snow White dance, humming to herself. The winter sun shone through the high windows and its beams lay round her like spotlights. She had not the slightest idea that she had an audience until someone suddenly coughed and she looked round to see Barbara and Belinda in the doorway.

She joined them hastily, blushing and disconcerted.

"I'll be late for French. But the floor looked so tempting."

"We didn't know you could dance like that!"

"I did tell you I'd learned."

"But you looked really good to us. Better than that stuck-up Candida. Why, you were like a real ballerina!"

"Oh, rubbish!" said Drina, still embarrassed. "I'm miles and miles off being a ballerina."

"How furious Candida would be if she knew! She thinks she's the only ballerina in this school."

"Well, don't tell her – please!" said Drina, and then she started rapidly in the direction of her classroom.

After that, they seemed to respect as well as like her, which struck Drina as odd when they mostly only admired skill in riding and skating.

But she was rather pleased, all the same, that they thought of her as a dancer.

More and more she was realising that she must tackle her grandmother, confess about Adele Whiteway and explain that it was no good trying to stop her dancing. It was the thing she just had to do.

"Born to be a dancer", Jenny had said. Drina still wondered sometimes about her mother, but she had not found out any more and it seemed as though she would not until her grandmother chose to explain, which she might not do until she was grown up.

"I shall *have* to make her listen to me," Drina

thought often, but she kept on putting off the occasion.

As November passed, she went several times a week to Miss Whiteway's. Adele was not always there, but Drina did not mind that, though she enjoyed their usually brief interesting conversations. Once or twice she met Lena, a well-built girl with red hair, and liked her very much. She would have liked to stay and listen for hours to Lena's tales of the Dominick School, but of course she could not, with her grandmother growing rather anxious now that the afternoons were so dark, even though she came home in a taxi.

So November went and the days of December were cold and windy, though sometimes sunny. A fortnight before Christmas, there was heavy frost and the lake in St. James's Park was covered with ice. The skating enthusiasts at the Pakington School were out all day Saturday and most of Sunday, but Drina refused to join them. She could not skate and would have felt silly amongst so many clever performers. But on the Sunday afternoon her grandfather produced some new skates and took her up to Hampstead Heath to learn. He was quite a good skater himself and soon had Drina, with her dancer's balance, skimming along beside him.

"You ought to go to an ice rink. You'd soon be very good," he said enthusiastically.

Drina returned home with glowing cheeks and a huge appetite, having really enjoyed her time on the ice. It *would* be fun to learn properly, she thought, but there would never be time. Because, at any rate by the New Year, she would have tackled her grandmother and begged her to arrange dancing lessons again, or an audition at one of the famous Ballet Schools.

It could not be put off much longer. She could not bear to dance to her own shadow for many more weeks.

# 5

# The Christmas Play

Christmas drew near very quickly and, in spite of the problem hanging over her, Drina's spirits were very high. It was fun to see the decorations going up in Regent Street and in the big shops, and it was exciting to watch – as she was lucky enough to do – the arrival of the huge Christmas tree in Trafalgar Square.

The weather was cold and frosty, which added to the growing Christmas atmosphere.

On the Saturday before Christmas, she went shopping with her grandmother, but they were separated for part of the time. Drina enjoyed being alone, pushing her way through the laden crowds. She had saved up to buy her presents, but had been much helped by some money pushed into her hand by her grandfather that morning.

"It's not your Christmas present, mind; it's just to help you to get all those expensive cards and calendars I know you want to get for your friends."

So Drina felt wealthy and was able to buy just the cards and calendars that she liked best. For Jenny's present she bought a delightful little picture of a farm scene, handkerchiefs for her grandfather and delicately perfumed soap for her grandmother. Jane, Barbara and Belinda were more difficult, but she ended by getting them each a calendar with tear-off pictures of horses.

Miss Whiteway she left till last and in the end bought her soap as well, of the make and perfume that she liked best.

Drina and her grandmother met again at the front entrance of the store and they had tea at a restaurant in Regent Street. It was almost dark by then and Drina was enchanted with the effect of the glittering, floating decorations overhead and with the brilliant lights on the many Christmas trees.

She spent Sunday parcelling up her presents and went back to school on the Monday in high spirits. School actually finished at Tuesday lunchtime, but there was to be a dress rehearsal of the play on Tuesday afternoon and the performance was to be given on the Wednesday evening, the day before Christmas Eve.

There was not much work done on Tuesday morning; it was more a matter of clearing up and tidying desks and cupboards. The girls had plenty of time to talk about their holiday plans and some of their chatter Drina found very interesting. Several lucky girls were going to Switzerland and Austria for the winter sports and one was flying all the way to the Far East to visit her parents. She lived with an aunt in London during term time.

Drina's own plans were much more ordinary, but she was looking forward greatly to visits to the theatre and to Jenny's arrival on January 4th for ten whole days.

The girls dashed up and down stairs in a way usually forbidden and even sang. The members of the staff, busy themselves, smiled and left them alone, so long as there was not too much noise.

Candida Selcourt, a little more aloof than usual because she thought herself quite the most important person in the play, had her usual admirers round her most of the time and was regaling them with the story of the show that had taken place at her Ballet School the previous night.

"And there was someone in the audience who asked quite loudly, 'Who is that lovely dancer with the curly black hair?'" she said triumphantly. "I got quite a lot of flowers, though of course Madame doesn't like me and never gives me a really good role."

"Oh, Candida!" cried one of the admirers. "And when you dance so beautifully! Why, you dance absolutely marvellously in our play. I've told Mother that you're the only one worth seeing."

"Oh well, of course I give my life to dancing," said Candida loftily, as the little group moved towards the stairs that led to the cloakrooms.

"Just fancy that!" said Belinda, sotto voce. She and her friends were not far behind.

"I'm *always* thinking about it," Candida went on, doing a ballet movement on the top step. "Mother said yesterday, 'I believe you dance in your sleep, Candida!' And really it's true. I *feel* myself dancing all the time, even going down the stairs."

It was just at that moment that a group of juniors arrived rather excitedly and almost collided with the little crowd above her. One of Candida's friends, taken unawares, missed her footing on the top step and grasped at Candida, immediately below. Candida, who had been holding a graceful position, gave a sudden yell, tried to seize the rail, missed it and fell down several stairs with a considerable clatter.

There was a horrified silence, in which Barbara's voice rang out:

"*Now* you've done it, girls! She's broken her neck for sure!"

The slightly older girls who had been listening to Candida had already gone anxiously down to her, jostling each other. Candida was sitting awkwardly about halfway down the stairs, her face white with pain.

"Better get Miss Drake!" said Belinda, who was always practical, and she flew off for help.

"I – I'll be all right in a minute," Candida said breathlessly. "I've just twisted my knee a little. What on earth happened, you clumsy things?"

"Some of the kids knocked into Sally and she grabbed at you. Oh, Candida, are you really hurt?"

"I don't know," said Candida, very much subdued. "I think the pain's going off."

But when two members of the staff came to help her to the Matron's room she could hardly walk and her knee was already beginning to swell.

"But the play? What about the play?" someone asked.

"We'll have to see about that later," said Miss Drake, the producer. "You'd better all get off home now, girls, and be back prompt at two. If the worst comes to the worst, the dance can be cut, I suppose, but it would be a great pity. What on earth made Candida fall?"

"She was doing ballet-dancing on the stairs," said Jane.

"Then she's a very silly girl and thoughtless, too. She knew how much we were counting on that dance. There's no understudy, of course. No one else learns ballet dancing and, anyway, Candida's never been away for a day since she started school."

"But there is someone else who dances!" said Belinda, from the heart of the little group.

Miss Drake looked startled and interested, and Drina dug Belinda in the ribs with her elbow.

"Shut up!"

"I won't shut up!" said Belinda clearly. "Miss Drake ought to know. It's a really good play and a pity to spoil it. Miss Drake, Drina Adams dances beautifully. She learned from someone who used to be with the Royal Ballet."

"Where is Drina?" Miss Drake's eyes searched the group and finally picked out Drina's small, rather shrinking figure. "Come here, dear. The rest of you get off, please. We don't want to be late starting the rehearsal. And remember, the costumes have to be complete, shoes and everything."

Drina advanced towards her with a bumping heart, feeling shy and rather silly.

"I – I did learn ballet for two years, but –"

"Well, I had no idea. Why didn't you say so? We might have fitted in another dance, even though you're new. Still, it's just as well we didn't, because we're going to need you as the Black Swan, I feel sure. We've sent for the doctor and Candida's knee looks quite bad to me."

"Oh, but –"

"You'd be willing to help us, wouldn't you? It wouldn't matter very much if it was a difference dance."

"I could do Candida's dance. I've watched her often," Drina confessed. "But –"

often," Drina confessed. "But –"

"Oh, my dear child, no buts! If you've learned dancing for two years you ought to be fairly good and I don't want the play spoilt by cutting out the Black Swan. It would be difficult to do so, really. Can you bring your shoes this afternoon? And we must send someone home in a taxi with Candida to borrow her costume. Her mother won't mind when it's a question of saving the play. It will be too big for you, of course, but someone will alter it tonight."

"I – I don't know if my grandmother will let me," Drina got out.

"Well, I'm sure she won't refuse to let you help if it's necessary. If you come to my room I'll write her a note."

So Drina, dazed and startled, found herself for the second time going home with a note. But this time she did not tear it up. She handed it to her grandmother immediately and burst into an explanation.

"Candida's hurt her knee and they don't think she'll be able to dance in the play. No one else can dance, so Miss Drake wants me to be the Black Swan. Oh, Granny! Please say I can do it! I'd love to, and Miss Drake will mind dreadfully if I let them down."

Mrs Chester read the note, frowning.

"How did this Miss Drake know you'd learned dancing?"

"Belinda knew and she told her when Candida fell. Oh, Granny!"

"Well, I must say I'd like to refuse. You're out of practice and I don't see how you can take someone else's part almost at a moment's notice."

"But I've watched her often. I can do her dance. It's really very easy, but the play would be spoilt without it."

Mrs Chester approved of the Pakington School and had no wish to get a reputation for awkwardness, but she was deeply dismayed. It was the last thing that she would have wanted to happen.

"Then I suppose I'll have to agree."

Drina immediately glowed with happiness.

"Oh, thank you, Granny!"

She ate a hurried lunch and then went to find a pair of ballet shoes. Two pairs were at Miss Whiteway's, but she had another nearly new pair that would do very well. She put them in her case with her peasant child's costume. Perhaps someone else would wear that – one of the understudies – or else her own unimportant part could be cut out altogether.

When she got back to school there was news of Candida. She was in considerable pain and would certainly not be able to dance, though there was no serious damage to the knee.

"Oh, poor Candida!" cried Drina, with real sympathy. she could still remember her own bitter disappointment when she caught mumps on the day when she should have danced in the Summer Show at the Selswick.

The Black Swan costume was there and she put it on. It certainly was rather too large, but not so much as might have been expected. It was a delightful costume and she looked strangely unfamiliar when she stared at herself in the mirror.

"I hardly know you, Drina!" cried Belinda, very pleased that her friend was going to dance.

The cloakrooms were filled with a whirl of activity

and the many costumes were very vivid.

"Why, Drina!" said Miss Drake, appearing amongst them. "That Swan costume doesn't fit too badly. I'll get Matron to look at it later and see where it needs taking in. She's promised to do it tonight. Everyone in the hall in five minutes, please!"

Once the curtain went up, Drina found that she was not at all nervous. It was all fun and very satisfying and she had little real doubt that she would acquit herself at least adequately as the Black Swan. She watched the first half of the play from the front and really enjoyed it, though there were one or two delays and setbacks. Then it was nearly time for her entrance and she slipped up the steps and into the wings.

The Black Swan music started and Drina moved on to the stage. In a sudden hush, she began to dance. Actually it was not the first time that she had done Candida's dance, for she had tried it once at Miss Whiteway's, having found a suitable record.

Soon she was enjoying herself thoroughly and had forgotten everything but the fact that she *was* a swan. The applause at the end surprised her and brought her sharply to earth. Even Miss Drake was clapping in the wings.

"That was beautiful, Drina! I can see you've been hiding your talents since you came to us. All right, carry on with the play, girls. Drina, you can run off to Matron's room and then go home if you like. We shan't want you again till tomorrow night, and thank you very much for helping us out."

Drina spent the evening and most of the following day in a sort of dream. She knew that her grandmother was not quite her usual self, and once or twice her heart sank. If Granny minded so very much that she was to dance in a school play, what hope was there of her agreeing to lessons again and forgiving her for the weeks of deception?

But that could not be dealt with yet – perhaps not until after Christmas.

Mr and Mrs Chester were to go to the play, but Drina had to be there early. Her grandfather sent her off in a taxi, telling her that they would follow in plenty of time to take their seats before the curtain went up.

"Good luck, Drina dear!" he said, as Drina settled into the dark interior of the taxi.

It was very satisfying and thrilling to find herself being made up again and to have the feeling of an impending show. It was an excitement that she had missed very much, though of course her dancing had mostly consisted of hard work and endless practising and there had been very few shows.

The hall was quite filled with parents and friends of the girls by five to seven, and, peering through the curtain, Drina could see her grandmother's well-arranged grey hair in the middle of the second row.

The play was a success almost from the start. It was very cheerful and colourful and there were some good actresses amongst the girls. Then came the dance of the Black Swan and Drina skimmed on to the stage in the soft black costume, her hair held closely to her head by a little cap of black feathers.

She danced as perhaps she had never danced before, for now she knew, as she had not known when she was Snow White, that she must savour every moment. How long would it be before she could really dance again?

At the end, she sank down near the footlights and then rose again slowly to make her exit. There was a storm of applause and some cries of "Encore!" but the play had to go on. She danced away into the wings and was captured by Miss Drake.

"I'm no judge, of course, but you seem extraordinarily good to me. Are you planning to make dancing your career?"

"I want to, Miss Drake," Drina said, still rather dazed. "But my – my grandmother isn't keen."

"Well, of course it's a hard and difficult life in some ways, but I should think your grandmother will have to change her mind. Thank you very much for helping us and giving us such a treat."

Drina went away to change and was ready to help to hand round coffee at the end of the play, before the end of term speeches and the brief prizegiving. The main prizegiving was always at the end of the summer term.

Many people spoke to her, praising her dancing, and even the older girls stopped to congratulate her and ask if she meant to be a dancer. It was very satisfying and exciting in some ways, but Drina was conscious of her grandmother's slightly grim presence.

Mrs Chester had merely said, "Very nice, Drina. I'm sure they're grateful to you for stepping into the breach."

Her grandfather had squeezed her hand and said that she had danced well, but she knew that they would both have preferred her not to dance and the knowledge upset her even more than usual.

They bore her off as soon as they could, and Drina knew without being told that they were anxious to avoid speaking to the headmistress.

Altogether it was a depressing end to such a successful evening, and she went to bed very soberly.

"It's no good! I don't believe Granny will change her mind, but I've *got* to talk to her. Perhaps I will tomorrow."

# 6

# Unexpected Meeting

**B**ut the next day, Christmas Eve, her grandmother was very busy, too busy to be inveigled into a long and difficult talk. She also seemed in an unusually thoughtful mood, for her brow was creased and she seemed not to have heard several things that were said to her.

Yet she did not seem to be annoyed with Drina; she was actually especially kind at times.

She went out to do some last minute shopping in the afternoon and Drina slipped away to Miss Whiteway's. Miss Whiteway was out, so she got·on with her practising, but just as she had finished and was changing back into her ordinary clothes, the door opened and Miss Whiteway looked into the studio.

She immediately invited Drina to stay for a cup of tea, and Drina did so, glad to have a chance to tell her all about the school play and how she had danced the Black Swan at the last moment.

Miss Whiteway seemed very interested, and she was delighted with her present, too. She gave Drina a beautiful newly published ballet book.

"I suppose I shan't be seeing you for a few days? Well, have a very good time, and after Christmas I hope to meet your grandmother. When is she going to arrange an audition for you?"

And Drina mumbled that she didn't know and flew off into the darkening streets of Westminster. In every way, it was beginning to be imperative to confess to Miss Whiteway and her grandmother, but she resolved now to leave it till after Christmas.

She had to hide the ballet book, of course, which added to her usual sense of guilt, but by evening she had really forgotten everything but the delights of Christmas. It was a frosty evening, with a brilliant young moon, and her grandfather took her to Trafalgar Square to join in the carol-singing round the lighted tree. It was a new experience for Drina, and one that she enjoyed very much. She looked round the Square wonderingly, thinking how strange it was that she should be a Londoner now and quite familiar with the fountains and the lions and the frontage of the National Gallery opposite.

> "See amid the winter snow,
> Born to us on earth below –"

Christmas really was the lovliest time of the year. Drina looked up at the little moon and then at the quiet, dark London buildings all round. How Jenny would have liked to be there to sing by the Christmas tree!

> "Good King Wenceslas looked out
> On the feast of Stephen,
> When the snow lay round about,
> Deep and crisp and even,"

sang Drina with the crowd, but her thoughts were suddenly far away as she looked back down the months of that eventful year. So much had happened, some things pleasant and exciting and some that she preferred not to remember. It was certainly better not to think about the hours that had followed the Summer Show, when she learned that her whole life was changing.

Well, it *had* changed, anyway, and, however guiltily and secretly, she was still dancing. But she wanted to dance with her grandparents' approval – wanted it with her whole heart.

"I think we ought to go. It's very late," said Mr Chester, and steered Drina through the crowd. They paused on the edge of the Square, before walking down Whitehall, and suddenly happiness and a sense of magic flooded Drina's whole being. How silly to remember problems when London lay under a little Christmas moon and people were singing carols round a gaily decked tree!

Christmas was altogether a happy time. Drina went to the Abbey on Christmas morning with her grandfather, and in the afternoon they all three walked into St James's Park and watched the children with their new toys. On Boxing Day they went to see a musical, which Drina enjoyed, though there was no actual ballet in it.

For some time now, she had been seeing posters advertising the current ballet season at the Royal Opera House, Covent Garden, but she knew that there was little hope of seeing the Royal Ballet Company, unless perhaps Jenny would say that she was longing to go. Jenny would do that for her friend, Drina knew, though probably she would prefer an ordinary musical or a play. Anyway, there would be a concert on the night after she arrived; Mr Chester had bought the tickets for that some time before.

After Christmas, Drina had a sense of flatness, interspersed with moments of sharp anxiety and excitement. She waited for an opportunity to bring up the subject of dancing, but did not receive one.

She awoke four days after Christmas with a feeling of acute depression and, lying there in her pretty little room, had no means of knowing that it was going to be a momentous day, the beginning of yet another part of her life.

She helped her grandmother about the flat in the morning, and then, in the afternoon, Mrs Chester said, "I want to walk along to the Army and Navy Stores to buy a new dress, Drina. Suppose you come with me? It will give you something to do."

Drina nodded and ran to put on her outdoor clothes. She would have preferred to go along to Miss Whiteway's to practise, but somehow it was easier to agree to her grandmother's suggestion.

So they walked briskly towards Victoria Street and were soon entering the big store where Mrs Chester did a good deal of her shopping.

Drina had had a good deal of money amongst her Christmas presents and was intending to buy some books. She thought perhaps she might slip up to the book department and look round, but her grandmother had other ideas.

"You had better come along with me. I shan't be very long, probably, and then I want to look at the china."

So Drina went with her to the dress department and meekly held her gloves and bag while various smart dresses were tried on. Mrs Chester chose one that she liked eventually, and, while it was being packed up, she turned to Drina to say:

"I think perhaps *you* might have a new dress for best. What do you think?"

But Drina was not listening. She was staring in fascinated horror at an advancing figure: a smartly dressed, familiar figure with slight limp. It was Miss Whiteway!

Miss Whiteway had seen her and was advancing, smiling.

"Hullo, Drina! How nice to see you again. Did you have a good Christmas? And is this your grandmother?" She turned to Mrs Chester and said pleasantly. "I've been wanting to meet you for some time, Mrs Chester. I've enjoyed having Drina come to me these last few weeks, but it's really time that she had proper dancing lessons again, as I'm sure you agree."

Mrs Chester was looking surprised and not best pleased.

"I'm afraid I have no idea who you are. Perhaps Drina will introduce us?"

But Drina was staring blankly, sick with dismay.

Miss Whiteway said, still smiling, though her eyes were alert, "I'm Adele Whiteway. You remember that I sent you a note asking if Drina might practise in my studio?"

"I received no note," answered Mrs Chester, with great dignity. "And I know nothing about Drina's practising. As far as I am aware she has scarcely danced since last July." Then she looked at Drina, who was gulping and suddenly hot and sick. "Drina dear, what is this? Miss Whiteway must think me very rude indeed, but I simply don't understand. Suppose you explain to us both."

"Oh, Granny, I – it's – I have meant to tell you, but – but –" and to her horror Drina felt tears rising to her eyes. She blinked them back, but they gathered faster than ever. She did not realise it, but the long weeks of strain had told on her and now, in the moment of crisis, she could not cope with life at all.

"I – I –" she tried again, but it was no good. She burst into tears.

Mrs Chester was deeply horrified.

"My dear Drina, kindly pull yourself together at once. A girl of your age can't cry in a public place." She took the dress-bag from the interested assistant and then turned to Miss Whiteway. "If you have no objection I think we had better go to the restaurant and sort this whole business out over a cup of tea."

"Yes, I'd be glad to," said Adele Whiteway, still rather puzzled, but beginning to realise the importance of the situation.

"Then let us hurry. Dry your eyes at once, Drina."

Drina did her best but soon found herself urged into the ladies' room by her grandmother.

"Wash your face and compose yourself and then come and join us."

Drina obeyed, taking rather a long time, and when she went towards the corner table her grandmother and Miss Whiteway were deep in conversation.

Drina dropped into a chair and said wretchedly, "Granny, I *did* mean to tell you as soon as I got the courage. I always felt awfully bad about it, but I couldn't help myself. I just *have* to dance, and Miss Whiteway has been so kind. I know it was awful to tear up the note and her uncle the Canon's telephone number, but I couldn't bear you to say no."

Mrs Chester had learned a good deal during her absence and, to Drina's relief, seemed to have taken to Miss Whiteway. She said briefly to her granddaughter, "Keep quiet for a little, please, Drina, and let Miss Whiteway finish telling me about you."

Adele Whiteway gave Drina a reassuring look and continued to speak of Drina's practising, of her own career as a dancer and a designer, and of her belief that

Drina had the makings of a really good dancer. At the end, Mrs Chester gave a little sigh and leaned back in her chair.

"Thank you for being so frank with me. Drina was very wrong to put us both in this difficult situation, and certainly she should not have been so deceitful. But I do see – and have been seeing for some time – that I have been quite wrong. It goes very much against the grain with me to admit that, but I hope I am an honest woman. I honestly believed that it was better for Drina not to dance, but I can see now that one can't fight against the inevitable and I shan't fight any longer."

"Granny!" gasped Drina, feeling as though she had never seen her grandmother before.

The tea came and Mrs Chester poured out three cups before going on; then she said, "You think that Drina has talent. Well, I know that she has, too, only I hoped against hope –"

"I think she has more than talent, though it's early to say."

"Quite so. Twelve is far too young to know, but sometimes there are signs. I know enough to realise that."

"Granny!" Drina cried again, astonished and unbelieving.

"I think that she ought to have the best possible training, Mrs Chester, but it's not really my business. You don't know me –"

"But you know Drina, and you've been helping her. I'll be frank with you, Miss Whiteway. It seems the only thing now, and Drina had better understand, too. I wouldn't have chosen this time and place, but since it has happened like this – well, perhaps it's as well. I was putting off making the decision I knew I would have to make. You see, all these years I've fought against seeing another child go into the world of ballet."

Drina was only staring now, and Miss Whiteway preserved an interested silence, looking levelly into Mrs Chester's face.

"I never meant Drina to dance at all, but she began to do so when she was very small. Very soon she was demanding lessons, and gradually circumstances forced me to let her have them. I hoped against hope that she would lose her enthusiasm, especially when she found that ballet is hard work and leaves little time for anything else. But she didn't seem to mind the work at all; in fact, she revelled in it. I didn't really see her dance for nearly two years after she started training and then I realised that the decision I had taken some weeks earlier might be the only way of stopping her making dancing her career. I saw that she was good and that there would soon be no chance whatever of stopping her, and I wanted her to give up dancing more than I wanted anything else in the world. Partly because I believed that it would be for her own good, and partly because I felt I couldn't face going back myself into that world that I once, most unwillingly, had to inhabit to a certain extent."

"My mother —" said Drina with a gasp, and Mrs Chester nodded. She went on:

"The decision that we had taken was to come and live in London again. My husband had been offered an excellent job here and I hoped that Drina, away from the Selswick school and her old friends, would find new interests. Instead she kept straight on with her dancing, as best she could. I saw her dance a few nights ago and knew that she was better than ever, though I had no idea then that she had kept up her practising. So now I give in and, as soon as possible, I'll arrange for her to have an audition at one of the well-known schools."

Drina gasped again, but Adele Whiteway gave her a warning glance.

"And it was Drina's mother who – led you into the world of ballet?"

"Yes. I can't imagine where she got it from. There was no one who danced in my family, nor in my husband's. But she showed talent at an early age and she got a scholarship to a ballet school when she was eleven. I never really liked it or approved, though we were both proud of her in a way, of course. She did very well and would have done better if she had not died young. I took Drina and we moved from London, and – well, you know the rest."

"Yes," said Miss Whiteway, very thoughtfully. "Yes. I see. And I do sympathise with you. But some things are impossible to stop and I think that Drina must dance."

"Yes, she must. I shan't stand in her way any longer."

"Oh, thank you, Granny!" Drina cried, rather chokily, and Mrs Chester, suddenly brisk, said tartly:

"Don't let us have any more tears, please, Drina. You've got your wish and I and your grandfather will help you all we can. He always said I was wrong to try and stop you, though he isn't eager for you to be a dancer. And, of course, there is always the chance that you won't be good enough when you're older."

"But I will work! I'll work terribly hard," said Drina.

"What about the Igor Dominick School?" asked Miss Whiteway.

"I'll think about what will be best and perhaps we could meet again? If you could come and have tea with

us on New Year's Day we might discuss the matter
further."

"I should like that very much," said Adele
Whiteway. "I'm most anxious to help all I can."

"Thank you. You know the address? We'll expect
you about four o'clock. And now we'd really better go.
Come, Drina!"

Drina said goodbye to Miss Whiteway and followed
her grandmother in a complete daze. She was to have
her wish; she was to be a dancer, as her mother had
been before her. Her mother!

"Will you tell me about my mother?" she asked, as
they walked back along Victoria Street in the blue
December dusk.

Mrs Chester glanced down at the little figure by her
side.

"Yes, one day soon. But not yet. Get used to one
thing first. There are photographs and things you can
see."

"Oh, Granny, I am so sorry about not telling you
things! I did truly feel most terribly bad."

"I'm sorry you deceived me, but perhaps it was my
fault," Mrs Chester said, and they walked on through a
world suddenly filled with bells, in an atmosphere of
better understanding than they had known for a very
long time.

# 7

# Two Tickets for Covent Garden

Nothing much was said that evening before Drina went to bed and, as a matter of fact, she went to bed very early. She was heavy and headachy after the emotional afternoon, so Mrs Chester packed her off and brought her hot milk when she was undressed.

"Now don't lie there thinking about things. Get a good sleep. You're going to have your wish and there's no further need to worry."

"I'll try, Granny," Drina said meekly, and she drank the milk and curled up contentedly in her narrow bed. She slept almost at once and Big Ben was striking nine before she awoke.

After breakfast, Mrs Chester said:

"Why don't you go out for a walk this morning? It's a lovely day, though very cold."

So Drina put on her coat and the big fur-lined gloves that had been her grandfather's Christmas present. She took her purse, too, just in case she came back past any bookshops.

She paused for a short while on Westminster Bridge, but the wind was too cold for lingering. So she returned to the Embankment and strode rapidly towards Waterloo

Bridge, her heavy hair blown back from her face and her cheeks beginning to glow.

Seagulls wheeled and cried over the grey water, reminding her suddenly and vividly of the coasts of Western Scotland and the Lleyn Peninsula where there had been so many seabirds. Perhaps, next summer, she would ask to be taken back to one of them.

She walked so fast that she soon reached Waterloo Bridge, and then she turned towards the Strand, with some idea of making her way back to Trafalgar Square and then across St James's Park. But she had not gone far when she caught sight of a poster and the words "Royal Opera House" sprang out at her. It was a programme for the current season. There would be opera that night, but the next evening there was ballet. Ballet at Covent Garden on New Year's Eve. Tomorrow!

Drina stood stock still in the middle of the crowded pavement, and a little man, pushing past her, said amiably enough. "Nar then! Nar then! Bin struck all of a heap?"

It was true enough, too. Drina had been struck by a daring idea. In her purse she had all her Christmas money – quite a vast amount. Was there the faintest hope that if she went up to the Royal Opera House she might get two seats for the ballet? If she *did* manage to get them then surely her grandmother would go with her – now?

But there probably wasn't any hope at such a late date, though she remembered hearing her grandfather speak more than once of getting "returns" for the theatre. "Returns" were tickets that people handed back at the last moment because they had found they couldn't use them.

Her heart was beating wildly by this time and her hands were clammy with excitement and hope. She had never seen the Royal Opera House, but was sure that it was not far away from where she stood.

A policeman was standing on the corner and she retraced her steps to ask hesitantly. "Please can you tell me the way to the Royal Opera House?"

The policeman looked down at her, smiling.

"Want to go to the opera?"

"No, the ballet," Drina said earnestly.

"Well, cross over and keep straight on up Wellington Street. You'll soon see it on your left."

"Oh, thank you very much!" And Drina waited till the traffic stopped and bounded over the crossing. But as she continued up Wellington Street she walked more and more slowly. Just now, not knowing whether she would get seats or not, she could savour the hope. In five minutes she might have no hope at all, and suddenly she was on fire with eagerness to see the Royal Ballet and the greatest of all ballerinas.

When she saw the huge building in front of her her heart quickened, though her footsteps did not. A notice told her that the booking-office was in Floral Street on the other side of the Opera House.

A few people were going in and out. Drina, suddenly very shy and extremely doubtful of herself, pushed open the door and found herself in warm brightness. It was the first time she had ever tried to book theatre seats and she began to feel very small and very young.

There were three people in front of her at the booking-office, the window of which was very high, so that Drina wondered if she would be able to see over the top when she got closer. A tall, prosperous-looking man was putting down a wad of notes to pay for a box and Drina envied him and his party fiercely. Lucky, lucky people, who were sure to see *Les Sylphides*,

*Daphnis and Chloe* and *Les Patineurs* the following night!

The man immediately in front of her was paying for a box, too. Drina stared blankly into the middle of his back and tried to will the cheerful young man in the box office to find her two seats.

It was her turn and she stood on tiptoe, looking up at him. At first, in her intense eagerness, no words would come; then she gasped out "Oh, please, I suppose you haven't – are there *any* seats for tomorrow night?"

"How many do you want?"

"Oh, two."

Though she had nerved herself to hear the words "No, I'm sorry. There aren't any seats!" they did not come. The young man's face disappeared, and she stood stiffly on tiptoe, her hand clutching all the money she had on the ledge above her.

After what seemed like a long time the young man's face was back again.

"The only seats there are, are two in the Stalls Circle." He was showing her on the plan and Drina craned her neck.

"They're rather at the side, but quite good seats. And they're all I have."

"Oh, thank you! I'll take them," said Drina, almost unable to believe her good luck. She took the envelope marked "Royal Opera House" and stumbled out into the cold sunshine again. Some way down the street she stood still and looked at the tickets, waves of excitement running up her spine.

She was going to see the Royal Ballet, and on the wonderful opening night that she had read about, when the people in the audience wore gorgeous dresses, and flowers were presented to the most famous dancers! Above all, she was going to see first-class ballet for the very first time.

She put the tickets away in her purse and somehow got herself down the Strand. She had enough sense left to dive down the steps and cross Trafalgar Square underground. Otherwise, in her dazed state, she would probably have got run over and would never have seen the ballet at all.

She arrived back at the flat starry-eyed and almost incoherent with excitement. She babbled so much that Mrs Chester said quite gently:

"Now start again, Drina! I haven't grasped it yet. What ballet have you got tickets for?"

"Oh, Granny, for the Royal Ballet tomorrow night at Covent Garden! For the opening night! I just can't believe it! Oh, Granny you *will* come with me? I shall die if you won't."

Mrs Chester said dryly:

"There's no need to die, Drina. Since you've been lucky enough to get seats of course I will come. It's a good thing that you've got that new dress. We shall need to dress up."

"And Grandfather won't mind, will he? I only had enough money for two tickets, and anyway, there weren't any more seats."

"No, I don't suppose he'll mind. As a matter of fact, he rang up yesterday evening to try and get seats for us, but there were none at all. You must have got 'returns'. What a lucky girl you are!"

So Drina was in the seventh heaven and her grandmother sighed because she could get so little sense out of her for the rest of the day.

Drina scarcely knew how she would live until it was time to go to the ballet, but Mrs Chester was determined to keep her occupied. In the morning they went shopping and in the afternoon they went to the wintry Zoo, where Drina forgot a little of her restless excitement in watching the antics of the monkeys and the strange writhings of the snakes in the Reptile House.

The Zoo closed early, of course, so they returned to the West End and had tea, returning to the flat in good time to dress for the theatre.

Drina's new dress was white and quite the most grown up one she had ever had. To add to her feeling of elegance she had a little scarlet cape to put round her shoulders and a small scarlet evening bag to hold her handkerchief and comb.

Mr Chester took them to Covent Garden in the car, but pointed out that they would have to come back by taxi, as he had no idea what time the ballet would be over. Drina sat alone in the back of the car, warmly wrapped up in her best coat and a fluffy rug and, as she looked out at the evening glitter of London, she could hardly believe that she was really Drina Adams on her way to see the Royal Ballet.

Mr Chester drew up in front of the Opera House, in

the midst of all the arriving and departing taxis, and Drina caught glimpses of figures in evening dress and pressmen hurrying about with cameras. There was flash after flash as photographs were taken.

"Have a good time!" called Mr Chester, as he began to drive away, and Mrs Chester led Drina firmly inside, into the glare of lights and the company of a crowd of beautifully dressed people. She seemed to know her way about very well and led Drina quickly round the back of the auditorium to the cloakroom.

"Oh, Granny, you've been here before!" Drina said breathlessly, trying to take in the vast building.

"Of course I have. Hurry up and take your coat off, Drina. There's going to be a crowd in here very soon."

So Drina handed her coat and gloves to the attendant and combed her hair. Then she arranged the cape and, catching a glimpse of herself in the long mirror, was astonished to see that she looked almost pretty. She usually thought of herself as rather plain, but there was no doubt that tonight she looked quite striking. Probably it was the brilliant scarlet so close to her dark hair and eyes.

Their seats certainly were at the side, but they were at the front of the Stalls Circle and she knew that she would be able to see most of the great stage. It was thrilling to watch the people arriving, but quite soon she buried herself in her programme, drinking in the famous names and reading the story of *Daphnis and Chloe*, though she already knew it.

Mrs Chester sat there calmly, staring about her. Once she gave a little bow to someone in the stalls just below them, and Drina, noticing, asked:

"Who is he, Granny? Isn't he handsome?"

"Colin Amberdown, the ballet critic."

"Oh, but – he writes books about ballet, too. I read

his *Our Changing British Ballet* not long ago."

"Did you indeed?" said her grandmother, with a small, half-amused smile. "I should think you found it fairly heavy-going?"

"Oh, it wasn't! Not a bit. I loved it."

"He's heart and soul in the ballet world, and he has some connection with the Dominick School."

It was nearly half-past seven. Drina was tense with excitement as she looked round the vast place. She had once seen it on television, but she had scarcely been prepared for its hugeness.

"I am at Covent Garden!" she told herself. "I am here at the opening night." But she could scarcely believe it.

She still did not believe it when the music of *Les Sylphides* began and the curtain rose on the grouped white-clad figures. How long ago it seemed since she sat in the shabby old Grand Theatre with Mrs Pilgrim and Jenny, watching this same ballet! But she knew now that the company she had seen had indeed been third-rate and, watching the perfection of the dancing on this far greater stage, she was filled with so great a delight that her eyelids prickled.

Her whole being seemed to follow the familiar music and it was as though she was there in spirit with those airy dancers, who had most of them left the anxious, hard years of training behind them. Though she knew, of course, that even the ballerina, at the height of her power, must still practice every day of her life.

Sitting there at Covent Garden, for the most part lost and entranced, Drina vowed at the very back of her mind that, if it was possible by years of hard work, she would somehow try to achieve perfection. It might not be possible, of course, but she would try.

And then she forgot everything else but the ballet before her.

# 8

# The Whole Truth

At the end of *Les Sylphides*, Drina came very slowly back to earth and began to clap with the rest of that huge audience. The curtain rose and fell again and again and the ballerina was presented with great sheaves of flowers. She smiled and curtsied, but the audience would not let her go.

"But don't imagine yourself in that position," said Mrs Chester, in her dry, rather tart way. "If you stick to your dancing and make it your career, there'll be years of being in the *corps de ballet* and after that you may never be a ballerina."

"Oh, Granny, I know," Drina said, blinking. "I've always known, I think. But I don't really care. Even just to be in the *corps de ballet* in a really good company! I think that would make me happy."

"I hope you will be happy," said her grandmother. "As I've told you, it's not my idea of a good life. That's why I didn't want it for you. Now I think we'll stay here during this interval and then after *Daphnis and Chloe* we'll go up into the 'Crush Bar'. You'll like to see the chandeliers and all the people."

After that she did not speak again and Drina sat there in a dream, keyed up to what was to follow. For she had still to see the greatest ballerina of the present day, who was only dancing in the main ballet. *Prima*

*Ballerina Assoluta*! Of all the titles in the world that seemed to her the most satisfying.

She was very tense as the curtain went up, revealing the scene that she had seen sometimes in pictures: "*Before the Cave of the Nymphs.*"

The shepherds and shepherdesses arrived to present their offerings before the nymphs of Pan and Drina stiffened to such tenseness as she watched Chloe that her back ached, though she did not realise it till afterwards. The great ballerina, as Chloe, looked so very, very young in her simple dress, and oh! the delight of her every perfect movement. It seemed to Drina as she watched that long ballet that she might never see anything so beautiful and moving again. She wanted it never to end, so that she could stay in that lovely, brilliantly-coloured world, knowing such utter delight.

But the third scene ended almost before she expected it and she was left with a tear in one eye that threatened to roll down her cheek, and yet it simply mustn't, as she dared not cry over dancing before her grandmother.

The curtains, the flower-giving, the wild clapping, seemed to last for a very long time, and through it all the great dancer remained smiling and serene – almost, thought Drina, a very young girl. And yet no young girl could have that wonderful poise and assurance. All the same, it was impossible to believe that she was quite old; well over thirty.

The curtain came down for the last time and Drina felt almost worn out. It was really a good thing that her grandmother was so matter of fact.

"Yes, well, it's not a ballet that appeals to me much, but you've certainly seen some perfect dancing. Now come along quickly, or we shall never get into the Crush Bar at all."

She bustled Drina up some stairs, along the top of a brilliantly lighted staircase and into a vast room, a-glitter with chandeliers and crowded with people, mostly in evening dress. They were thronging everywhere, all talking about the ballet and some clutching coffee cups. Drina hoped that her grandmother wouldn't insist on getting her coffee, because she was sure she would disgrace herself by dropping the cup. There was scarcely room to move.

Mrs Chester *did* insist on just that.

"I think you'd better have coffee. Go and stand by that pillar and I'll go and fetch it. Don't move, or I shall never find you again."

"No, Granny," Drina said meekly and she retreated obediently through the crowd to the pillar.

Mrs Chester brought two cups eventually and Drina was glad that they were in a fairly safe corner. She had drunk a little of the coffee when a male voice said close to her:

"I was hoping to get a chance to speak to you, Mrs Chester. It's many a long year since I saw you at an occasion like this!"

"Indeed it is, Mr Amberdown," agreed Drina's grandmother. "I've not been near any performance of ballet since that night when *The Breton Wedding* was first danced. I've had no occasion to, and I need hardly tell you that I've been glad."

"You never cared for the ballet," he said. His manner was – well, it was a strange word, but Drina thought dazedly that he sounded respectful. Why on earth should the great Colin Amberdown be respectful to her grandmother, especially when she had just said what must be heresy to him?

Mr Amberdown's calm grey eyes looked down at Drina.

"And is this – your granddaughter? Don't tell me that you're bringing her to see ballet at last?"

"Yes, this is Andrina. And actually she brought *me*," said Mrs Chester, with a faint chuckle. "Marched up here by herself yesterday and came back with two tickets."

"Hum! So it's come out, after all, has it? I know you said she should never have anything to do with the ballet."

"I said a lot of things and meant them," said Mrs Chester grimly. "But it wasn't a bit of good. Drina found ballet for herself. She insisted on learning from Janetta Selswick, and now she's made me agree to letting her have an audition at one of the Schools. But we only decided two days ago, and I've made no plans yet. I suppose, though, that it will be the Dominick School."

Drina was very shy and rather puzzled under the searching eyes. Why was he so interested in her?

"I should think it will have to be, considering that they helped to make her mother what she was. And, God knows, they'll jump at the chance of taking Ivory's daughter."

The great chandeliers seemed to be descending on Drina in a blaze of light. The crowd seemed to her to have gone silent; the world was rocking. She heard her grandmother say:

"Take her coffee cup, for heaven's sake! She didn't know."

"Didn't know what?" asked Colin Amberdown, taking the cup with one hand and putting the other arm behind Drina, who was grateful for the support. Things were still whirling about in the most alarming way.

"That her mother was Elizabeth Ivory. I was always afraid that she'd get hold of the 'Life' and guess. She could hardly fail to have done. She reads so many ballet books, and I suppose there might have been something in any one of them, but —"

Things were getting back to normal, but Drina still felt hot and weak. She opened her eyes wide and stared at them.

"My mother – oh, it *can't* be true! I thought she was in the *corps de ballet* in some third-rate company!"

"I didn't tell her that," said Mrs Chester hastily. "I didn't tell her anything. But I was going to do so tomorrow."

"Your mother," said Mr Amberdown very clearly, "was Elizabeth Ivory of the Igor Dominick Company. She was one of the most wonderful dancers that Britain will ever see, even greater, some think, than this great dancer we have seen tonight. She died very young, of course, but even so –"

"How did she – die?" Drina asked.

"Well, she was flying to the States to appear as a guest artist with an American company in New York and the plane crashed. You must have read that."

"Yes, I – have. But I didn't know – I can't believe –"

"Your grandmother, who had never wanted her to be a dancer, felt that dancing had led to her death. Wasn't that so?" he asked, quite gently.

Mrs Chester said dryly:

"Yes, it was true. I always hated all that travelling that Betsy had to do. New York, Paris, Stockholm, Helsinki. Once she was famous we scarcely saw her, though she was always a loving daughter as far as she could be. Even her husband and baby scarcely saw her."

"But she couldn't help it. Dancers have to do that," said Drina. She had not yet really taken in the wonderful news. She still felt very wavering and odd.

"There's the bell. We'll have to go," said Colin Amberdown. "Well, let me know what you decide and I'll arrange it for you with the Dominick School."

"Mr Amberdown!" cried Drina, clutching his sleeve.

"Yes?" He hesitated, looking down at her.

"Mr Amberdown, I – I haven't had time to think yet, but I know one thing *now*. Please don't tell them – Don't tell *anyone* – that I'm Ivory's daughter."

The crowd was streaming past, but he stopped dead. His eyes had lit up with quick understanding, though Mrs Chester looked startled and a trifle annoyed.

"Drina, don't be ridiculous! Why –"

"Because – because I want to be quite on my own. To work as *me*; not as Ivory's daughter. I don't want things made easy for me. I don't want people to say, 'Take her because she's Ivory's daughter!' Later they can know, if I'm good, but not now. You do understand?"

"Yes, and they shan't know," Mr Amberdown assured her. Then he patted her arm briefly and went away.

"Well, you are a strange child!" said Mrs Chester, as they made their way back to their seats. "But you're certainly like your mother. *She* was always independent and knew her own mind. I should have thought you'd want to shout from the house-tops that Elizabeth Ivory was your mother!"

"I do! I do!" Drina cried. "But I shan't – not yet. Oh, Granny, promise that you won't tell anyone. Not even Miss Whiteway? It's enough that *we* know!"

"I promise," said Mrs Chester, with a very faint smile, and ushered her into her seat.

After that the last ballet was rather lost on Drina. She was still too amazed, too happy, too unbelieving. *Ivory!* Of all the great dancers of the past and present Ivory had been her mother!

She knew that she would never, as long as she lived, forget those moments under the chandeliers, when she had learned the whole truth.

It was nearly a quarter to eleven when they came out into a cold, brilliant world. A nearly full moon was shining over London and the air was crisp with frost.

There seemed to be no taxis available near the Royal Opera House and Mrs Chester walked Drina briskly towards the Strand.

"I expect we'll get one soon, and, meanwhile, it may clear your head to walk for a little, Drina. You've got your warm coat on and can't get cold."

"Yes, I'd like to walk. Oh, Granny! In not much more than an hour it will be the New Year!"

"I expect people will be getting excited in the Square," said Mrs Chester, without enthusiasm.

"Oh, *can't* we walk as far as there? I've never been in London at New Year before. And – and I don't want to go home yet."

They walked rapidly down the Strand, and, as they approached Trafalgar Square, they saw that people were gathering already. Some wore paper hats and carried balloons, and quite a number of groups were too riotous for Mrs Chester's taste.

"I never *can* see why people have to get drunk before they can be cheerful!"

"I wish we could stay till midnight!" said Drina, ignoring the laughing youths and staring eagerly across the road towards the lions and the fountains.

"Well, we certainly can't. Your grandfather would be frantic with worry. Look! Here's a taxi!"

As the taxi drew up Drina took a last look at Trafalgar Square and the excited people; then she was deep in the stuffy gloom and they were soon flying off down Whitehall.

Mr Chester was waiting with sherry for himself and

his wife and hot milk for Drina, but Mrs Chester said most uncharacteristically:

"Wait till midnight and then let Drina have just a few drops of sherry. After all, it's been a wonderful night for her. Even I must admit that the ballet was superlative, and we met Colin Amberdown. He told her that her mother was Elizabeth Ivory."

"I can't believe it yet!" said Drina, crouching on the rug.

"And Drina told him that if she goes to the Dominick School she doesn't want anyone to know about her mother. She wants to stand or fall by her own efforts."

"Good for Drina!" said her grandfather warmly.

"So it's to be a secret, Grandfather! A wonderful secret just for us. Mr Amberdown has promised not to tell anyone at all, and I'm sure he's the sort of person who keeps promises."

"But other people will guess. Plenty of people saw your grandmother in the old days, and then there's your name."

"I could be plain Drina Adams, – at first, anyway. Even Madame never guessed, though she knew my name was Adamo."

"Your mother's marriage had very little publicity. She wanted it that way. She was always Ivory, so perhaps her married name didn't register with people. But people certainly may recognise me at the Dominick School," said Mrs Chester. "I took Betsy there for her audition and I was there off and on for years after that."

"Well, perhaps – someone else could take me to the audition. Would you mind?"

"Mind? No," said Mrs Chester, to whom that other occasion when she had accompanied the eleven-year-old Betsy was still a vivid memory. "I expect Miss

Whiteway would take you. She seems very' interested in you, and I must admit that I'd sooner not go."

Drina sat looking up at her grandmother.

"What was it like – taking my mother?"

"She was just eleven. She had reddish hair and was rather thin and pale. She wasn't an especially promising little dancer, but she was quite convinced that she must dance. I think it was more her determination than any very obvious talent that got her that scholarship to the Dominick School. But there's no need for you to worry about a scholarship. Your mother, as well as your father, left you a great deal of money."

They talked in a desultory fashion, with Drina nibbling biscuits until a few minutes before midnight. Then, as the bells began to rock the air all about them, Mr Chester poured out two glasses of sherry and a little one for Drina.

"Let us drink to the New Year and to Drina's future!"

Drina did not like the sherry much, but she gulped it down. It was midnight! It was the New Year! A wonderful, wonderful New Year, full of hope!

The bells and the hooters on the river were still sounding as she went to her room. She flung the window wide and leaned out into the moonlight.

London! she thought. London! Lovely, lovely city!

Then she shut the windows again, and, shivering, began to fling off her clothes. She was in bed and almost asleep when her grandmother came to tuck her up and kiss her.

"Good night, dear!"

"Tomorrow – tomorrow I can see all the pictures of my mother?"

"Yes, tomorrow," said Mrs Chester, and went away.